HORSES I'VE KNOWN

With desperate effort, he'd bought out his wickedest jumps to of no use.

HORSES
I'VE KNOWN

By
WILL JAMES

Mountain Press Publishing Company
Missoula, Montana
2004

First Printing, April 2004

*Tumbleweed is a registered trademark of
Mountain Press Publishing Company*

Library of Congress Cataloging-in-Publication Data

James, Will, 1892–1942.
Horses I've known / Will James.
      p.   cm. — (Tumbleweed series)
ISBN 0-87842-493-8 (cloth : alk. paper) — ISBN 0-87842-494-6
(pbk. : alk. paper)
1. Horses—Fiction   I. Title.
PS3519.A5298H67 2004
813'.52–dc22

                                                                2004005937

PRINTED IN THE UNITED STATES OF AMERICA

Mountain Press Publishing Company
P.O. Box 2399 • Missoula, Montana 59806
(406) 728-1900

To the memory of a mighty fine man and friend,

ELROY WESTBROOK,

I dedicate this book.

BOOKS BY WILL JAMES

Cowboys North and South, 1924

The Drifting Cowboy, 1925

Smoky, the Cowhorse, 1926

Cow Country, 1927

Sand, 1929

Lone Cowboy, 1930

Sun Up, 1931

Big-Enough, 1931

Uncle Bill, 1932

All in the Day's Riding, 1933

The Three Mustangeers, 1933

Home Ranch, 1935

Young Cowboy, 1935

In the Saddle with Uncle Bill, 1935

Scorpion, 1936

Cowboy in the Making, 1937

Flint Spears, 1938

Look-See with Uncle Bill, 1938

The Will James Cowboy Book, 1938

The Dark Horse, 1939

Horses I've Known, 1940

My First Horse, 1940

The American Cowboy, 1942

Will James Book of Cowboy Stories, 1951

PUBLISHER'S NOTE

WILL JAMES'S BOOKS are an American treasure. His writing and draw-ings captivated generations of readers with the lifestyle and spirit of the American cowboy and the West. Following James's death in 1942, the reputation of this remarkable writer and artist languished, and nearly all of his twenty-four books went out of print. But in recent years, publication of sev-eral biographies and film documentaries on James, public exhibitions of his art, and the formation of the Will James Society have renewed interest in his work.

Now, in conjunction with the Will James Art Company, Mountain Press is reprinting all Will James's books under the name Tumbleweed Series, taking special care to keep each volume faithful to the original. Books in the Tumble-weed Series contain all the original artwork and text, feature an attractive new design, and are printed on acid-free paper.

Will James wrote his stories many years ago, long before the term *politically correct* entered our lexicon. *Horses I've Known* contains a few incidents that, if viewed through today's critical lens, would be deemed biased or insensitive. As with other great early-twentieth-century writers, James needs to be read with a mind to the era in which he wrote.

The republication of Will James's books would not have been possible with-out the help and support of the many fans of Will James. Because all James's books and artwork remain under copyright protection, the Will James Art Company has been instrumental in providing the necessary permissions and furnishing artwork.

The Will James Society was formed in 1992 as a nonprofit organization dedicated to preserving the memory and works of Will James. The society is one of the primary catalysts behind a growing interest not only in Will James and his work, but also in the life and heritage of the working cowboy. For more informa-tion on the society, contact:

Will James Society • c/o Will James Art Company
2237 Rosewyn Lane • Billings, Montana 59102

Mountain Press is pleased to make Will James's books available again. Read and enjoy!

JOHN RIMEL

PREFACE

Here's a whole book on some of the horses I've known. I wrote of these special ones because they sort of stand out in character, traits, peculiar, good or ornery ways, from many others I've known.

As horses go, none are alike in character, and even tho some colts might be from the same mother and father, alike in color and markings, none will be alike in thinking and acting, just as it is with human families or with crowds.

The bad might come out of the best, and the other way around. The horses in this book are each of a different character, from good to just plain tricky and bad, each in their own way, to keep his rider at ease or guessing.

There's young and even a couple of old pensioners, none of no account in their own way, and I think they're well worth telling of in these pages. I wish I could tell of 'em as I really knew 'em and have the reader feel the same as I did with my experiences with them by this writing and drawings of 'em.

But I think the reader will get a fair idea, and maybe see as I do, a sort of likeness to the human in their faithfulness, or trickery or scheming bad or good acting, all in their different ways.

CONTENTS

ILLUSTRATIONS

HORSES I'VE KNOWN

I

THE SEEING EYE

I<small>T'S WORSE THAN TOUGH</small> for anybody to be blind but I don't think it's as tough for an indoor born and raised person as it is for one whose life is with the all out-of-doors the most of his life from childhood on. The outdoor man misses his freedom to roam over the hills and the sight of 'em ever changing. A canary would die outside his cage but a free-born eagle would dwindle away inside of one.

Dane Gruger was very much of an out-of-door man. He was born on a little ranch along a creek bottom, in the heart of the cow country, growed up with it to be a good cowboy, then, like with his dad, went on in the cow business. A railroad went thru the lower part of the ranch but stations and little towns was over twenty miles away either way.

He had a nice little spread when I went to work for him, was married and had two boys who done some of the riding. I'd been riding for Dane for quite a few days before I knew he was blind, not totally blind, but, as his boys told me, he couldn't see any further than his outstretched hand, and that was blurred. He couldn't read, not even big print, with any kind of glasses so he never wore any.

That's what fooled me, and he could look you "right square in the eye" while talking to you. What was more he'd go straight down to the corral, catch his horse, saddle him and ride away like any man

1

with full sight. The thing I first noticed and wondered at was that he never rode with us, and after the boys told me, I could understand. It was that he'd be of no use out on the range and away from the ranch.

Dane had been blind a few years when I come there and he'd of course got to know every foot of the ten miles which the ranch covered on the creek bottom before that happened. The ranch itself was one to two miles wide in some places and taking in some brakes. The whole of that was fenced and cross-fenced into pastures and hay lands, and Dane knew to within an inch when he came to every fence, gate or creek crossing. He knew how many head of cattle or horses might be in each pasture, how all was faring, when some broke out or some broke in, and where. He could find bogged cattle, cow with young calf needing help, and know everything that went well or wrong with what stock would be held on the ranch.

He of course seldom could do much towards helping whatever stock needed it or fix the holes he found in the fences, but when he'd get back to the ranch house he could easy tell the boys when there was anything wrong, and the exact spot where, in which field or pasture, how far from which side of the creek or what fence and what all the trouble might be. It would then be up to the boys to set things to rights, and after Dane's description of the spot it was easy found.

During the time I was with that little outfit I got to know Dane pretty well, well enough to see that I don't think he could of lived if he hadn't been able to do what he was doing. He was so full of life and gumption and so appreciating of all around him that he could feel, hear and breathe in. I'd sometimes see him hold his horse to a standstill while he only listened to birds or the faraway bellering of cattle, even to the yapping of prairie dogs which most cowboys would rather not hear the sound of.

To take him away from all of that, the open air, the feel of his saddle and horse under him and set him on a chair to do nothing but sit and babble and think, would of brought a quick end to him.

With the riding he done he felt satisfied he was doing something worth doing instead of just plain riding. He wouldn't of cared for that, and fact was he well took the place of an average rider.

But he had mighty good help in the work he was doing, and that was the two horses he used, for they was both as well trained to his wants and care as the dogs that's used nowadays to lead the blind and which are called "The Seeing Eye."

Dane had the advantage of the man with the dog, for he didn't have to walk and use a cane at every step. He rode, and he had more confidence in his horses' every step than he had in his own, even if he could of seen well. As horses do, they naturally sensed every foot of the earth under 'em without ever looking down at it, during sunlight, darkness or under drifted snow.

Riding into clumps of willows or thickets which the creek bottoms had much of, either of the two horses was careful to pick out a wide enough trail thru so their rider wouldn't get scratched or brushed off. If they come to a place where the brush was too thick and Dane was wanting to go thru that certain thicket, the ponies, regardless of his wants, would turn back for a ways and look for a better opening. Dane never argued with 'em at such times. He would just sort of head 'em where he wanted to go and they'd do the rest to pick out the best way there.

Them horses was still young when I got to that outfit, seven and eight years of age, and would be fit for at least twenty years more with the little riding and good care they was getting. Dane's boys had broke 'em especially for their dad's use that way and they'd done a fine job of it.

One of the horses, a gray of about a thousand pounds, was called Little Eagle. That little horse never missed a thing in sight, or sound. With his training the rustling of the brush close by would make him investigate and learn the cause before leaving that spot. Dane would know by his actions whether it was a new-born calf that had been hid or some cow in distress. It was the same at the boggy places along the creek or alkali swamps. If Little Eagle rode right on around and without stopping, Dane knew that all was well. If he stopped at any certain spot, bowed his neck and snorted low, then Dane knew that some horse or cow was in trouble. Keeping his hand on Little Eagle's neck he'd have him go on, and by the bend of that horse's neck as he went, like pointing, Dane could tell the exact location of where that animal was that was in trouble, or whatever it was that was wrong.

Sometimes, Little Eagle would line out on a trot, of his own accord and as tho there was something needed looking into right away. At times he'd even break into a lope, and then Dane wouldn't know what to expect, whether it was stock breaking thru a fence, milling around an animal that was down, or what. But most always it would be when a bunch of stock, horses or cattle would be stringing out in single file, maybe going to water or some other part of the pasture.

At such times, Little Eagle would get just close enough to the stock so Dane could count 'em by the sound of the hoofs going by, a near impossible thing to do for a man that can see, but Dane got so he could do it and get a mighty close count on what stock was in each pasture that way. Close enough so he could tell if any had got out or others got in.

With the horses in the pastures, there was bells on the leaders of every bunch and some on one of every little bunch that sort of held together and separate from others. Dane knew by the sound of every bell which bunch it was and about how many there would be to each. The boys kept him posted on that every time they'd run a bunch in for some reason or other. Not many horses was ever kept under fence, but there was quite a few of the purebred cattle for the upbreeding of the outside herds.

At this work of keeping tab on stock, Little Eagle was a cowboy by himself. With his natural intellect so developed as to what was wanted of him, he could near tell of what stock was wanted or not and where they belonged. The proof of that was when he turned a bunch of cattle out of a hayfield one time, and other times, and drove 'em to the gate of the field where they'd broke out of, circled around 'em when the gate was reached and went to it for Dane to open. He then drove the cattle thru, none got away, not from Little Eagle, and Dane would always prepare to ride at such times, for if any did try to break away Little Eagle would be right on their tail to bring 'em back, and for a blind man, not knowing when his horse is going to break into a sudden run, stop or turn, that's kind of hard riding, on a good cowhorse.

About all Dane would have to go by most of the time was the feel of the top muscles on Little Eagle's neck, and he got to know by them about the same as like language to him. With one hand most always on them muscles he felt what the horse seen. Tenseness, wonder, danger, fear, relaxation and about all that a human feels at the sight of different things. Places, dangerous or smooth, trouble or peace.

Them top muscles told him more, and more plainly than if another rider had been riding constantly alongside of him and telling him right along of what he seen. That was another reason why Dane liked to ride alone. He felt more at ease, no confusion, and wasn't putting anybody out of their way by talking and describing when they maybe wouldn't feel like it.

And them two horses of Dane's, they not only took him wherever he wanted to go but never overlooked any work that needed to be done. They took it onto themselves to look for work which, being they always felt so good, was like play to them. Dane knew it when such times come and he then would let 'em go as they chose.

Neither of the horses would of course go out by themselves without a rider and do that work. They wouldn't of been interested doing that without Dane's company. What's more they couldn't have opened the gates that had to be gone thru, and besides they wasn't wanted to do that. They was to be the company of Dane and with him in whatever he wanted to do.

Dane's other horse was a trim bay about the same size as Little Eagle, and even tho just as good he had different ways about him. He was called Ferret, and a ferret he was for digging up and finding out things, like a cow with new-born calf or mare with colt, and he was even better than Little Eagle for finding holes in fences or where some was down.

All that came under the special training the boys had given him and Little Eagle, and if it wasn't for automobiles these days, such as

He was called Ferret, and a ferret he was for digging up and finding things.

them would be mighty valuable companions in the city, even more useful in the streets than the dog is, for the horse would soon know where his rider would want to go after being ridden such places a few times.

Unlike most horses it wasn't these two's nature to keep wanting to turn back to the ranch (home) when Dane would ride 'em away, and they wouldn't turn back until they knew the ride was over and it was time to. Sometimes Dane wouldn't show up for the noon meal, and that was all right with the ponies too, for he'd often get off of 'em and let 'em graze with reins dragging. There was no danger of either of them ever leaving Dane, for they seemed as attached to him as any dog could be to his master.

It was the same way with Dane for them, and he had more confidence in their trueness and senses than most humans have in one another.

A mighty good test and surprising outcome of that came one day as a powerful big cloudburst hit above the ranch a ways and left Dane acrost the creek from home. The creek had turned into churning wild waters the size of a big river in a few minutes, half a mile wide in some places and licking up close to the higher land where the ranch buildings and corrals was.

It kept on a-raining hard after the cloudburst had fell and it didn't act like it was going to let up for some time, and the wide river wouldn't be down to creek size or safe to cross, at least not for a day or so.

The noise of the rushing water was a-plenty to let Dane know of the cloudburst. It had come with a sudden roar and without a drop of warning, and Dane's horse, he was riding Little Eagle that day, plainly let him know the danger of the wide stretch of swirling fast waters. It wasn't the danger of the water only but uprooted trees and all kinds of heavy timber speeding along would make the crossing more than dangerous, not only dangerous but it would about mean certain death.

Little Eagle would of tackled the swollen waters or anything Dane would of wanted him to, but Dane knew a whole lot better than to make that wise horse go where he didn't want to, any time.

Dane could tell by the noise, and riding to the edge of the water and the location where he was, how wide the body of wild waters was. He knew that the stock could keep out of reach of it on either side without being jammed against the fences, but he got worried about the ranch, wondering if the waters had got up to the buildings. He worried too about his family worrying about him, and maybe try to find and get to him.

That worrying got him to figuring on ways of getting back. He sure couldn't stay where he was until the waters went down, not if he could help it. It wouldn't be comfortable being out so long in the heavy rain either, even if he did have his slicker on, and it wouldn't do to try to go to the neighbor's ranch which was some fifteen miles away. He doubted if he could find it anyway, for it was acrost a bunch of rolling hills, nothing to go by, and Little Eagle wouldn't know that *there* would be where Dane would be wanting him to go. Besides there was the thought of his family worrying so about him and maybe risking their lives in trying to find him.

He'd just have to get home, somehow, and it was at the thought of his neighbor's ranch and picturing the distance and country to it in his mind, that he thought of the railroad, for he would of had to cross it to get there, and then, thinking of the railroad, the thought came of the trestle crossing along it and over the creek. Maybe he could make that. That would be sort of a dangerous crossing too, but the more he thought of it the more he figured it worth taking the chances of trying. That was the only way of his getting on the other side of the high waters and back to the ranch.

The railroad and trestle was only about half a mile from where he now was and that made it all the more tempting to try. So, after thinking it over in every way, including the fact that he'd be taking chances with losing his horse also, he finally decided to take the chance, at the risk of both himself and his horse, that is if his horse seen it might be safe enough. He felt it had to be done and it could be done, and there went to show his faith and confidence in that Little Eagle horse of his.

And that confidence sure wasn't misplaced, for, a cooler-headed, brainier horse never was.

There was two fences to cross to get to the railroad and trestle, and it wasn't at all necessary to go thru gates to get there, for the swollen waters with jamming timbers had laid the fence down for quite a ways on both sides of the wide river, some of the wire strands to break and snap and coil all directions.

A strand of barbed wire, even if flat to the ground, is a mighty dangerous thing to ride over, for a horse might pick it up with a hoof, and, as most horses will scare, draw their hind legs up under 'em and act up. The result might be a wicked sawing wire cut at the joint by the hock, cutting veins and tendons and often crippling a horse for life. In such cases the rider is also very apt to get tangled up in the wire, for that wicked stuff seems to have the ways of the tentacles of a devilfish at such times.

Loose wire laying around on the ground is the cowboys' worst fear, especially so with Dane, for, as he couldn't see it was many times more threatening as he rode most every day from one fenced-in field to the other. But the confidence he had in his two cool-headed ponies relieved him of most all his fear of the dangerous barbed wire, and either one of 'em would stop and snort a little at the sight of a broken strand coiled to the ground. Dane knew what that meant and it always brought a chill to his spine. He'd get down off his saddle, feel around carefully in front of his horse, and usually the threatening coil would be found to within a foot or so of his horse's nose. The coil would then be pulled and fastened to the fence, to stay until a ranch hand who, with team and buckboard, would make the rounds of all fences every few months, done a general fixing of 'em.

It's too bad barbed wire *has* to be used for fences. It has butchered and killed many good horses, and some riders. But barbed wire is about the only kind of fence that will hold cattle, most of the time, and when there has to be many long miles of it, even with the smaller ranches, that's about the only kind of fence that can be afforded or used. Cattle (even the wildest) seldom get a scratch by it, even in breaking thru a four-strand fence of it, or going over it while it's loose and coiled on the ground, for they don't get rattled when in wire as a horse does, and they hold their hind legs straight back when going thru, while with the horse he draws 'em under him instead and goes to tearing around.

Both Little Eagle and Ferret had been well trained against scaring and fighting wire if they ever got into it, also trained not to get into it, and stop whenever coming to some that was loose on the ground.

That training had been done with a rope and a piece of smooth wire at one end, and being they was naturally cool-headed they soon learned all the tricks of the wire and how to behave when they come near any of that coiled on the ground.

There was many such coils as the flood waters rampaged along the creek bottom, and as Dane headed Little Eagle towards the railroad and trestle he then let him pick his own way thru and around the two fence entanglements on the way there, along the edge of the rushing water.

Little Eagle done considerable winding around and careful stepping as he come to the fences that had been snapped and washed to scattering, dangerous strands over the field, Dane gave him his time, let him go as he choose, and finally the roar of the waters against the high banks by the trestle came to his ears. It sounded as tho it was near up to the trestle, which he knew was plenty high, and that gave him a good idea of what a cloudburst it had been.

He then got mighty dubious about trying to cross the trestle, for it was a long one, there was no railing of any kind on the sides, and part of it might be under water or even washed away. There was some of the flood water in the ditch alongside the railroad grade and it wasn't so many feet up it to the track level.

Riding between the rails a short ways he come to where the trestle begin and there he stopped Little Eagle. The swirling waters made a mighty roar right there, and how he wished he could of been able to see then, more than any time since his blindness had overtook him.

Getting off Little Eagle there he felt his way along to the first ties to the trestle, of the space between each, which was about five inches, and just right for Little Eagle's small hoofs to slip in between, Dane thought. One such a slip would mean a broken leg, and the horse would have to be shot right there, to lay between the rails. The rider would be mighty likely to go over the side of the trestle, too.

Dane hardly had any fear for himself, but he did have for Little Eagle. Not that he feared he would put a foot between the ties, for that little horse was too wise, cool-headed and careful to do anything like that, Dane knew. What worried him most was if the trestle was still up and above water all the way acrost. There would be no turning back, for in turning is when Little Eagle would be mighty liable to slip a hoof between the ties. The rain had let up but the wind was blowing hard and the tarred ties was slippery as soaped glass.

It all struck Dane as fool recklessness to try to cross on that long and narrow trestle at such a time, but he felt he should try, and to settle his dubiousness he now left it to Little Eagle and his good sense as to whether to tackle it or not.

If he went he would *ride* him across, not try to crawl, feel his way and lead him, for in leading the horse he wouldn't be apt to pay as much attention to his footing and to nosing every dangerous step he made. Besides, Dane kind of felt that if Little Eagle should go over the side he'd go with him.

So, getting into the saddle again, he let Little Eagle stand for a spell, at the same time letting him know that he wanted to cross the trestle, for him to size it up and see if it could be done. It was up to him, and the little gray well understood.

It might sound unbelievable, but a good sensible horse and rider have a sort of feel-language which is mighty plain between 'em, and when comes a particular dangerous spot the two can discuss the possibilities of getting over or acrost it as well as two humans can, and even better, for the horse has the instinct which the human lacks. He can tell danger where the human can't, and the same with the safety.

It was that way with Little Eagle and Dane, only even more so, because as Little Eagle, like Ferret, had been trained to realize Dane's affliction, cater and sort of take care of him, they was always watchful. Then with Dane's affection and care for them, talking to 'em and treating 'em like the true pardners they was, there was an understanding and trust between man and horse that's seldom seen between man and man.

Sitting in his saddle with his hand on Little Eagle's neck the two "discussed" the dangerous situation ahead in such a way that the loud roar of the water foaming by and under the trestle didn't interfere any with the decision that was to come.

There was a tenseness in the top muscles of Little Eagle's neck as he looked over the scary, narrow, steel-ribboned trail ahead, nervous at the so careful investigation, that all sure didn't look well. But he'd now left it all to Little Eagle's judgment, and as Dane had about expected he'd be against trying, Little Eagle, still all tense and quivering some, planted one foot on the first tie, and crouching a bit, all nerves and muscles steady, started on the way of the dangerous crossing.

Every step by step from the first seemed like a long minute to Dane. The brave little horse, his nose close to the ties, at the same time looking ahead, was mighty careful how he placed each front foot, and sure that the hind one would come up to the exact same

14

place afterwards, right where that front one had been. He didn't just plank his hoof and go on, but felt for a sure footing on the wet and slippery tarred ties before putting any weight on it and making another step. Something like a mountain climber feeling and making sure of his every hold while going on with his climbing.

The start wasn't the worst of the crossing. That begin to come as they went further along and nearer to the center. There, with the strong wind blowing broadside of 'em, the swift waters churning, sounding like to the level of the slippery ties would seem about scary enough to chill the marrow in any being. But there was more piled onto that, for as they neared the center it begin to tremble and sway as if by earth tremors. This was by the high rushing waters swirling around the tall and now submerged supporting timbers.

Little Eagle's step wasn't so sure then, and as careful as he was there come a few times when he slipped, and a time or two when a hoof went down between the ties, leaving him to stand on three shaking legs until he got his hoof up and on footing again.

With most any other horse it would of been the end of him and his rider right then. As it was, Little Eagle went on, like a tightrope walker, with every muscle at work. And Dane, riding mighty light on him, his heart up his throat at every slip or loss of footing, done his best not to get him off balance but help him that way when he thought he could.

If the shaking, trembling and swaying of the trestle had been steady it would of been less scary and some easier, but along with the strong vibrations of the trestle there'd sometimes come a big uprooted tree to smash into it at a forty-mile speed. There'd be a quiver all along the trestle at the impact. It would sway and bend dangerously, to ship back again as the tree would be washed under and on.

Such goings on would jar Little Eagle's footing to where he'd again slip a hoof between the ties, and Dane would pray, sometimes cuss a little. But the way Little Eagle handled his feet and every part of himself, sometimes on the tip of his toes, the sides of his hoofs and even to his knees, he somehow managed to keep right side up.

Good thing, Dane thought, that the horse wasn't shod, for shoes without sharp calks would of been much worse on than none on the slippery ties. As it was, and being his shoes had been pulled off only a couple of days before to ease his feet some between shoeings, his hoofs was sharp at the edges and toe, and that gave him more chance.

The scary and most dangerous part of the trestle was reached, the center, and it was a good thing maybe that Dane couldn't see while Little Eagle sort of juggled himself over that part, for the trestle had been under repair and some of the old ties had been taken away in a few places, to later be replaced by new ones; but where each tie had been taken away that left an opening of near two feet wide. Mighty scary for Little Eagle too, but he eased over them gaps without Dane knowing.

Dane felt as tho it was long weary miles and took about that much time to finally get past the center and most dangerous part of the five-hundred-yard trestle, for them five hundred yards put more wear on him during that time than five hundred miles would of.

And he was far from near safe going as yet, for he'd just passed center and the trestle was still doing some tall trembling and dangerous weaving, when, as bad and spooky as things already was, there come the sound of still worse fear and danger, and Dane's heart stood still. It was a train whistle he'd heard above the roar of the waters. It sounded like the train was coming his way, facing him, and there'd sure be no chance for him to turn and make it back, for he'd crossed over half of the trestle, the worst part, and going back would take a long time.

All the dangers and fears piling together now, instead of exciting Dane, seemed to cool and steady him, like having to face the worst and make the best of it. He rode right on towards the coming train.

He knew from memory that the railroad run a straight line to the trestle, that there was no railroad crossing nor other reason for the engineer to blow his whistle, unless it was for him, himself. Then it came to him that the engineer must of seen him on the trestle and would sure stop his train, if he could.

Standing up in his stirrups he raised his big black hat high as he could and waved it from side to side as a signal for the engineer to stop his train. Surely they could see that black hat of his and realize the predicament he was in. That getting off the trestle would mean almost certain death.

But the train sounded like it was coming right on, and at that Dane wondered if maybe it was coming too fast to be able to stop. He got a little panicky then, and for a second he was about to turn Little Eagle off the trestle and swim for it. It would of been a long and risky swim, maybe carried for miles down country before they could of reached either bank, and it would of taken more than luck to've succeeded. But if they'd got bowled over by some tree trunk and went down the churning waters that would be better, Dane thought, than to have Little Eagle smashed to smithereens by the locomotive. He had no thought for himself.

He rode right on towards the coming train.

About the only thing that made him take a bigger chance and ride on some more was that he knew that the whole train and its crew would be doomed before it got halfways on the trestle, and what if it was a passenger train?

At that thought he had no more fear of Little Eagle keeping his footing on the trestle. His fear now went for the many lives there might be on the train, and he sort of went wild and to waving his big black hat all the more in trying to warn of the danger.

But he didn't put on no such action as to unbalance the little gray in any way. He still felt and helped with his every careful step, and then there got to be a prayer with each one, like with the beads of the Rosary.

He rubbed his moist eyes and also prayed he could see, now of all times and if only just for this once, and then the train whistle blew again, so close this time that it sounded like it was on the trestle, like coming on, and being mighty near to him.—Dane had done his best, and now was his last and only chance to save Little Eagle and himself, by sliding off the trestle. He wiped his eyes like as tho to better see, and went to reining Little Eagle off the side of the trestle. But to his surprise, Little Eagle wouldn't respond to the rein. It was the first time excepting amongst the thick brush or bad creek crossings that horse had ever went against his wishes that way. But this was now very different, and puzzled, he tried him again and again, with no effect, and then, all at once, *he could see.*

MYSELF AND ONE OF DANE'S BOYS had been riding, looking for Dane soon after the cloudburst hit, and seeing the stopped passenger train

19

with the many people gathered by the engine we high-loped towards it, there to get the surprise of seeing Dane on Little Eagle on the trestle and carefully making each and every dangerous step towards us and solid ground.

We seen we sure couldn't be of no use to the little gray nor Dane only maybe a hindrance, and being there was only a little ways more we held our horses and watched. Looking on the length of the trestle we noticed that only the rails and ties showed above the high water, there was quite a bend in it from the swift and powerful pressure and the rails and ties was leaning, like threatening to break loose at any time.

How the little horse and Dane ever made it, with the strong wind, slippery ties and all a-weaving, was beyond us. So was it with the passengers who stood with gaping mouths and tense watching. What if they'd known that the rider had been blind while he made the dangerous crossing?

And as the engineer went on to tell the spellbound passengers how that man and horse on the trestle had saved all their lives, they was more than thankful, for, as the heavy cloudburst had come so sudden and hit in one spot, there'd been no report of it, and, as the engineer said, he might of drove onto the trestle a ways before knowing. Then it would of been too late.

But Little Eagle was the one who played the biggest part in stopping what would have been a terrible happening. He was the one who decided to make the dangerous crossing, the one who had to use his head and hoofs with all his skill and power, also the one who at the last of the stretch would not heed Dane's pull of the reins to slide off the trestle. His first time not to do as he was wanted to.

He'd disobeyed and had saved another life. He'd been "The See-ing Eye."

The fuss over with as Dane finally rode up on solid ground and near the engine, we then was the ones due for a big surprise. For Dane *spotted* us out from the crowd, and smiling, rode straight for us and looked us both "square in the eye."

The shock and years he lived crossing that trestle, then the puzzling over Little Eagle not wanting to turn at the touch of the rein had done the trick, had brought his sight back.

After that day, Little Eagle and Ferret was sort of neglected, neglected knee deep in clover, amongst good shade and where clear spring water run. The seeing eyes was partly closed in contentment.

II
JONES' BEARCAT

▾

MAYBE I SHOULDN'T TELL THIS story on account that the party I'm bringing in it might be sort of finicky if he gets wind that that story is spread around. But it won't hurt nothing only maybe his pride a little, and then I'm not going to mention the name he goes by nor the country he's located in. I'll just call him Jones, and as for the horse who figures in the story with him I'll start him out with the name of Socks. There's lots of Joneses and Socks.

I feel like I have a sure enough right to tell that story anyway because it's of a horse I broke myself, and it's the horse's actions mostly that go to make up the story.

Jones' outfit was one of the very few small outfits I ever came back to work for a second time, and I think that's saying a lot for it and Jones because I'd usually ride right on through small outfits so as to throw in with the big ones and where there was no danger of having to get off my horse to fix fence or any such like. Jones run about five thousand cattle; he handled the outfit himself and kept four or five riders pretty well the year around.

The first time I went to work for Jones was at breaking horses, and in the string of ten good broncs he'd cut out for me to break was this horse which in this story I later call Bearcat. That name wouldn't of fitted the bronc when I first broke him, and I'd named him Socks, just an ordinary name, for he behaved only like any other ordinary range bronc. (A bronc is an unbroken horse or one just started.)

He looked ordinary and fought and bucked the same, and while I was breaking him there was only one thing I noticed about him which was above ordinary and that caused me to sort of wake up sudden once in a while. That above-ordinary thing was the way he'd watch every move I'd make and got to planning ways of getting me down, in a pinch on the side of some steep hill, in the timber, or while I was watching a herd too close and him not close enough. He made me hunt for my "riggin" (saddle) quite a few times that way, and some of them times I thought I'd have to part with it. He was sure a mind reader as to when to try to get a feller, but maybe I was lucky, anyway he never got to lose me no time.

Yep, Socks had an over-ordinary set of brains, a lot of action and strength and speed, and I done my best to get him to use all of that in ways of learning neckrein and turning a fast-dodging steer. I wanted his little pin ears to point ahead and watch things that way instead of back and watching me for a good chance to tear loose and try to lose me. I'd have to sort of grin sometimes when he'd think I'd be napping and he'd be about to start something. I'd just show him my quirt to let him know I was very much awake, and being I'd made him well acquainted with that quirt at times when he deserved it, the sight of it would usually take all ornery notions out of his head right sudden, for he's seen that I couldn't be caught napping right then.

But it wasn't always that I would feel any kind of warning, and he'd often break in two before I had time to even twitch a muscle or

He was sure a mind reader as to when to try to get a feller.

prepare for a ride. A kind of hunch or instinct from riding many of his kind would work faster than my head about then, like as natural as blinking an eye before a hornet hits it and that instinct, or whatever it was, was what saved me from his slipping out from under me and leaving me in mid air quite a few times.

I'd rode Socks for a short time every day or so and along with the other broncs for about two weeks before I noticed that his ears begin to point other directions than back at me. He was taking other interest than to watch for a good time to try and buck out from under me, and every chance I got I'd point him to a herd where I'd put him to work a little at cutting out a few cattle.

In a couple of months I turned him and other broncs over as ready to go on with the regular work of handling cattle. Socks, like any ordinary bronc, had seemed to lose his ambitions to buck and went to work well. But as I gave him one more look when one of the riders come to take him and the other horses away to the round-up, I got the hunch that that pony would have to be watched some more. Not so much now but later on, after he'd been rode more and got wiser and then was turned loose for a few months. I would of liked to been around when he was caught again after that rest and had time to think things over. I knew from experience that a horse sure does think things over that way, most times to the good but sometimes to the bad, too, and according to his leaning.

As was usual with me, after I'd turn the broncs over as ready to work and drawed my money, I run in my private string of horses, all fat and fresh, and hit out for new territory where after some days I run onto the size outfit I liked to ride for. They was running three round-up wagons of about twenty riders and a two hundred saddle horse "remuda" to each, but with all that spread there was only two jobs open, one nighthawking (herding remuda at night) and the other riding the rough string (spoiled horses). I took the rough string.

I rode the rough string till the round-up was over and the wagons pulled in for the year, then I run in my fresh horses again and drifted on some more. I drifted on that way from one outfit to another for a couple of years, and then, not thinking much as to which way I was drifting one time, and only wanting to hit for high country, I seen one day where I'd just about made a circle in my drifting and was to within only a hundred miles of Jones' range, where I'd broke that Socks bronc a couple of years before, and forgot about him.

The way I come to realize that was how the cowboys of the outfit I was riding with at the time kept a-harping about some wampus-cat of an outlaw horse Jones had and which he dared any rider to try and set, betting it couldn't be done, and winning steady at it. The horse's name was Bearcat, and I didn't pay much attention to the name because there was many horses by that name and quite a few I'd given that name to myself. But I didn't recollect naming any bronc I'd broke for Jones, Bearcat.

Anyway, that Jones' Bearcat horse sure seemed to've made a rep for himself, and as he piled rider after rider, and that was spread around, he got to be the talk of every cow camp to within two hundred miles of Jones' country. As I went from outfit to outfit I got to hear plenty more about him, that Jones used that horse to tryout the riders he hired, but that he'd hire some that couldn't ride the horse on account that if he didn't he wouldn't have no riders. Of course the stories got to swell fit to bust as they was being repeated but I was satisfied from the first telling that that horse was sure worth riding some ways aside to see.

That had something to do with my drifting on to the Jones' range one fine spring day, and getting a job without the asking, for Jones had another string of broncs he wanted broke and I'd rode in just in time. I figured sure I was in for it right then and that that Bearcat horse would be throwed in the string for me to take the rough off of him. So, I was kind of surprised when my string was all cut out and in another corral, that the Bearcat horse wasn't among 'em, for I seen that the broncs I was to break was all "raw" ones. (Never been handled.)

Then out of the other horses, Jones pointed Bearcat out to me, began talking about him and asked if I remembered him. Sure, I remembered him, if not by his looks I would by them shifty pin ears of his. He was that ordinary bronc with the watchful eye, which I'd named Socks, the one always watching for a chance to catch me napping, or in a pinch before he would try to buck me off. He sure must of caught somebody napping a few times all right, and kept that up till he got scientific in his bucking. Now, as I was told, he didn't have to catch his men napping, he could twist a rider off of him any time or place and while that rider was well prepared to try and stay.

It had been as I'd expected might happen. The horse had been fine when I'd turned him over to the other riders, he'd been fine for some months after that and took to the handling of cattle like a right good one. When the work was done and he was turned loose for a few months and then caught up again he was still fine. He'd of course acted up and bucked a little but that's natural of any horse that's been broke only a short time, and even the old well-broke cowhorse will sometimes stir things up a-plenty when first rode after a long rest that way.

All might of been well and Socks might of turned out as a good cowhorse, on account he had the brains, but the rider who got him in his string when he was run in again got caught napping, that is he didn't have the knack of being up to whatever a horse might do right quick. He sort of had to be warned, and he was a pretty fair rider, but like some I know if he didn't see a horse's head under him, he was lost.

Consequences is, Socks bucked him off a few times, and then that horse, mighty pleased with himself, got more fun out of perfecting ways of getting out from under a rider than he did to turning the steer. That horse had got to using his good set of brains to bucking instead of cow work, and he done well at that. He was put in another rider's string then and his education only improved some more there, but in bucking, for he had to buck harder and better as the second man was a better rider than the first. Bearcat done well in getting rid of him too.

After that it was just a case of riders come, riders went. Very little cow work could be done with him, and when he was turned loose after the round-up was over and caught up again later on, he was ornery as any horse could be, and that's going some. He'd thought things over some more, and now it looked like Socks was out of the running for a good cowhorse. He was an ornery fighting wild cat, not just a plain crazy hardheaded bucker and outlaw that'd wear himself out fighting but a wise, cool-headed figuring cross between a whirlwind and a ton of brick.

After that it was just a case of riders come, riders went.

So the horse's name had been changed from ordinary Socks to Bearcat, the last being a heap more fitting. I didn't hanker for the horse to be cut to me, but I was there to line out any horse that was pointed out and I figured it would be sort of expected that I should ask for him. If I didn't it would hint that I was leary of him, so I did ask for him.

But Jones shook his head at that, and from the quick glance he gave me I got the sudden idea that he was afraid I would want to ride him, and that I *could.*

Well, that sort of pleased and relieved me all at once. I didn't want the horse in my string of broncs because I figured he was too far spoilt so as to get much good out of him unless a fellow rode the meanness out of him. That would take a lot of riding, mighty rough too, and then he'd be up to his old tricks again soon as he got rested up. Besides, with doing that I wouldn't have much time in a day to handle my other broncs, and that's where the money layed, for I was breaking them on contract and there'd be no breaking Bearcat now. He'd only be taking a lot of my time. I wondered, too, if I could ride him because he'd throwed some mighty good riders, and just to please myself and see if I could ride him I figured on trying him sometime, when nobody was around.

I went to work on the broncs and all was going fine, and I wasn't there at the headquarters ranch many days when I seen how Jones felt about Bearcat. Some of the boys would drop in from their different camps once in a while and tell me about it. How Jones was going around and using the name of Bearcat like a chip on his shoulder wherever he went, bragging about the horse and betting he couldn't be rode. He'd joke the life out of the good riders the horse had throwed, and when some rider would put up a good ride on a hard enough horse he'd remark that he hadn't rode a bucking horse yet, not until he'd rode that Bearcat horse of his.

Of course he done that all good-natured and in joking ways, but there was a strong sound of truth under his grinning remarks, and that didn't step by any of the riders. When in town once in a while, or in different camps or round-up wagons, he'd hear riders talk of Bearcat, of the men his horse had throwed and so on, he'd strut around like a peacock. He was sure proud of that horse and it would sure please him to hear his name mentioned and spread, along with his own name. Some of the riders figured that he'd rather parted with ten of his best cowhorses than he would Bearcat. Bearcat was of no use as a cowhorse and neither was he a top-notch race horse, but he was a champion in his line and Jones was proud that none had any better, or worse, and that the best riders had to bow to him.

I understood how Jones felt about Bearcat and why he didn't want him tamed down, for that horse was sort of his pride, and the way he'd watch over him, seeing he was always on the best of feed and in fine shape, kind of reminded me of a proud old eagle over one lone fighting youngster.

As time went on I got kind of anxious that some rider would come along and take a sitting on that horse; I wanted to see how he performed while I was on the ground and watching instead of up on him. I hadn't had much chance to try him myself because Jones stuck around pretty close, and anyway, I wasn't over-anxious to do that.

Then, like from an order, here comes a rider one day, the kind you could tell was a rider a mile away, no flashy outfit nor anything unnecessary on him or his horse but all about him and his simple riggin' was of the cut that marked him about a "waddy." He was a "ranahan," and the way he set his horse, even on a walk, I could see that he'd rode a-plenty and seldom on a broke horse. I had a hunch as he come to the corral where I was unsaddling a bronc that here was Jones', or Bearcat's Waterloo in person, and to make things all the more fitting he remarked as we got to talking that he was on the lookout for a job.

Him and Jones got together on the subject at the table that noon, and the stranger got the job. I'll call him Slim, for he was slim, and of average height. He would be initiated, as Jones put it, that afternoon, and on none other than Bearcat.

If it'd been me I'd been afraid to let that rider on that horse on account I figured he would sure ruin Bearcat's reputation for good, but Jones couldn't judge that rider for he'd only rode in one country and I could see that the whole West had been the rider's home, always a stranger and getting the rough end.

But it wasn't my funeral, and, as it was, I didn't get too far from the corral on the fresh bronc I proceeded to line out. I kept busy till the time when Bearcat was run in to try out his new victim, and I figured that this time, Bearcat was the most likely victim. I was sort of glad that Jones' other riders was all out to their scattered camps, for somehow I wouldn't of liked to've seen Bearcat's downfall witnessed by too many. There was just three of us and that was enough, Jones, Slim and myself.

Slim hardly looked at Bearcat till he flipped his rope on him, and then like it was just another horse. He saddled him in the same way, without any fuss and as tho he'd rode the horse many times before. A feller gets to know a horse mighty quick after he's handled a few thousand of 'em.

Bearcat didn't fight much as he was saddled, and he hardly quivered when the rider eased his foot in the stirrup to climb on him. The same wise horse, I thought, only wiser and saving himself for the right time as usual. His eyes and pin ears kept a-working, and I noticed that the rider noticed 'em, too. I figured right then that there was a match.

Slim slipped into the saddle, smooth as a cat reaching for a hunk of liver, and straight from the ground up all the time. He set his saddle the same and then slapped Bearcat's neck like as to say, "Let's go."

They went. Bearcat bogged his head, bellered like a mad cow and done some fast, high and crooked jumps, but he wasn't hitting the ground very hard and the rider took the jolts so easy that it looked like it wouldn't of been hard for him to eat a bowl of noodles with chopsticks while a-sitting up there. But even at that, Bearcat bucked hard enough to make it interesting for any average rider, and any average rider would also thought the horse was doing his best, too. But I knowed Bearcat when he was Socks, and I wasn't fooled.

Jones wasn't fooled either. I could tell that by the grin on his face when Bearcat raised his head and quit bucking. There'd be another spell coming.

Slim slapped him on the neck once more, and when Bearcat bowed his neck this second time he didn't do even as good as the first time. He just sort of crowhopped around and brought in only a few stiff jumps, and when he raised his head up again he started trotting around the corral, like he was all done with his bucking and was now ready to go to work.

The rider stopped him and grinned at Jones, like to ask if that was all. But Jones wasn't grinning this time, for he figured that *was* all.

"Hook him," he hollered. "He ain't started to——"

But he didn't get to say no more, for about that time, and while Slim was listening to Jones, Bearcat up and left the earth, and so sudden that Jones and me hardly got to see him go. He broke in two, and saddle strings popped while up there, and when he landed again, all twisted out of shape, it was like he'd been shoved back to earth by a falling meteor. He sure landed hard and crooked, but he didn't linger no time, and as he rebounded up again I sort of wondered how come his hide stuck to him.

Of course, Slim was mighty surprised with the first jump, for he'd about figured that Bearcat was through after the second bucking spell, and with that first unexpected hard jump he got loosened so that the earth didn't seem far away. His instinct or well-developed sixth sense at the unexpected that way is all that saved him from losing his riggin', and even though that riggin' was mighty hard to keep track of after that, he managed to straighten up in it, and ride.

Bearcat was now at his best and brought on every crooked jump that's possible for a horse to make, also many that seemed impossible, and there was no telling about any next jump, for there was no two alike and all a-purpose to puzzle and jar the eye teeth out of a rider. Slim had to use all of his skill. He rode straight up enough, and with his ability that way he sort of skipped many a jolt that would of sent a tight setting rider sailing, but he didn't bring on any extra action, such as scratching or fanning the horse, for there was plenty of action anyway and he was doing mighty well to just meet up with that.

It was nip and tuck between man and horse for a while, and then, after Bearcat brought on his best and seen that the rider was still on top and riding straight up, is when he sort of got desperate. He hadn't had a rider stick on him for so long for a long time. He'd brought on all his tricks, there was no more, and then he begin to lose his head. He was being rode sure enough, and that got him. He lost all sense of figuring ways to lose his rider and went to bucking wild, mad and reckless.

That only come easier for Slim, and then is when he begin to loosen up on some action of his own and begin "reefing" (scratching) Bearcat. The end soon come after that, for mad Bearcat's reckless bucking took his wind fast, and as a horse doesn't breathe in air while he's bucking, his hard hitting jumps soon dwindled to crowhops and then he finally came to a quivering standstill, the loser, and well ridden for that time.

Jones knew that Bearcat had done his best and bucked as hard if not harder than any time before. He felt very much the loser, and his pride in the horse, which was now gone, meant a heap more to him than any money he might of bet.

His face showed his feelings mighty strong as he watched the rider slide off Bearcat in that smooth and easy way of his and go to rolling a smoke. Then he walked over to him and without any howdedo, he blurts out, "You're fired."

Slim finished rolling his cigarette, lit it and then says, "I thought you'd hired me to *ride*."

"I did, but you done that too well. Now drift along, and take that horse with you. He's yours. I don't want him around. But don't let anybody know he's that Bearcat horse I had, understand?"

With that he turned on his way out of the corral and going past me he stopped only long enough to remark:

"And as for you, that horse is only Socks. You savvy, don't you?"

"Sure," I says, grinning.

And far as I know it's never been heard tell of that Bearcat horse ever being rode.

III

BORROWED HORSES

GRANT AND ME HADN'T BEEN to town for some months. We'd been riding, riding mighty hard for that wild outfit, the Square Cross ⊡, and being the work had slacked up some, the Fourth of July near and a rodeo was going to be pulled off in the town of Hardpan, a couple of days' ride away, we drawed our wages, saddled our private horses and rode in.

We was to within a few miles of town when, topping a low ridge, we come onto two horses. We'd rode on, only the appearance of them horses attracted us so we circled around and looked 'em over well. They was as pretty a pair of blacks as a man could wish to see, so well matched that they couldn't of been told apart, slick as seals, clean limbed and looked of good age.

They was plenty spooky acting but by taking it easy we got close enough to them to see faint collar marks on top of one of 'em's neck, no saddle marks, and trim and good size as they was that was a wonder to us, for both of 'em had the looks and makings of top saddle horses. Then we come to figure that them two being so well matched they'd been broke as a buggy team, and what a team they made.

That was in the days when a good-stepping, well-matched and pretty buggy team was noticed and admired as much, and more, than today's finest limousine or sports car.

We'd rode on, only the appearance of them horses attracted us so we circled around and looked 'em over well.

There was a very small brand on 'em, and reading it didn't tell us anything, for we didn't know who it belonged to, but I jotted it down in my tally book as is a habit when coming acrost likely stock that might of strayed away, for if sometimes some owner inquires, it's doing him a great favor to be able to inform him as to the where-abouts of whatever stock might of strayed away and got lost track of.

Always, in the feed stables, stock yards, post offices, and other places there was notices of stolen or strayed stock with rewards for information of their whereabouts or bringing them to their owners, and all range riders carried tally books where brands of likely look-ing stock which was thought might of strayed, was marked down, along with where they'd been seen, date, etc. That often came in mighty good stead to both finder and owner, and being the average cowboy covers hundreds of miles in many directions right along, sometimes into other states, he's a great help in locating strayed stock, and the tally books usually carries many brands and ear marks. It's up to the stock detective and sheriff to find whatever stock is stolen.

Riding on into town and to the feed stable where we put up our horses, we looked over the notices to see what there was of strayed or stolen stock but no notice was there for the two blacks nor for any we had down in our tally books. We marked down what stock was advertised on the notices and then we asked the stable man if he knew anything of the two blacks which we described to him and of who they might belong to.

He didn't know and nobody had mentioned 'em to him before. He didn't know the brand either and by that we got to thinking that the team must be strange or they'd sure been noticed and known, for that cow town wasn't so big, and everybody knew everybody else's horses. They sure would with such as the blacks, and so, they sure must of strayed from a long ways, we figured.

We didn't give 'em much more thought. Our main object for the time now was to get a few necessary new clothes, hit for the barber shop for a hair cut, on face as well as head, take a good bath and clean up in general, all in the same shop.

It took us a couple of hours but we was stinging clean and shining when we come out. The thing to do next was to take in the town, and being it was only a couple of days before the start of the three-day rodeo there was quite a few riders already come to compete in the contest, also many other people, such as cowmen and their families, and other kind, all for a good time and aiming to make it so.

The town was wide open and lively, and we took it in some. After months of hard riding it felt sort of good to mix in with many people for a change.

We did that, and getting along in the evening we then got thinking about a big T-Bone steak and trimmings, the kind we couldn't get at the round-up wagon, and we was starting away from the bar to go to a restaurant where we could get such a good order when we come face to face with an old cowman who'd rode with our outfit for a few days not long before then, looking for some of his stock. He had a nice little spread, running about a thousand cattle, and he informs us that he was giving a high jamboree dance at his home ranch on the next night and he'd sure like to have us come.

We was glad to accept and we'd sure be there, we said. His main ranch and home was only about eighteen miles from Hardpan and this town was where he done his trading. He was well known here, and being we was heading out to "throw a bait" (eat) we asked him if he'd come along, lead us to a good eating place and squat with us.

After a cordial appetizer or two he said he would, and soon enough we had our feet under a table and looking over a white table cloth. Quite a change from months of squatting on the ground with a tin plate between your knees.

The meal went mighty well as we talked. We was about thru, and the old cowman wanting another cup of black coffee after his dessert up and spoke to the waitress. He knew her.

"Millie," he says, "how would you like to go to a dance I'm giving tomorrow night at my Spring Creek Ranch?"

The girl smiled at him, then looked at us. "I'd love to," she says, "but I don't know if I can get away. I'll try and see and let you know later."

"Nothing doing." Comes back the old cowman. "If you'd like to come I'll see that you can get away, and your boss won't mind either. And," he went on, "could you get another likely girl like you to come along too? I'll talk to the boss to have somebody else to take your places for tomorrow night."

"Why," the girl thought some, "I guess I can. Maybe Mazie would come."

"Gemeny, that's fine," says the old cowman. Then pointing at us, he went on. "These two boys will bring you over and be your escorts, and I'll vouch for 'em as being as clean boys inside and out as you've ever met."

The girl sized us up a bit, smiled some and saying she'd let us know for sure the next day at noon, left us to stare after her and wondering. How in samhill was we going to take her and the other girl to the dance?

The old cowman took us so by surprise in getting the girls for us that we couldn't talk. When we did finally get so we could and asked him how in samhill we was going to take 'em to his shindig, he just shrugged his shoulders and grinned, remarking that a good cowboy can always overcome any obstacle.

By ourselves again we begin thinking on ways of taking the girls to the dance. We thought of our two saddle horses but right away dropped that idea, for they wasn't at all the kind that'd tolerate packing two riders at a time, and even if they would, the eighteen mile ride wouldn't do the girls' fancy dresses any good.

A good buggy and team would be the only thing. We went to the stable man about that and he had a two-seater democrat with canopy top which would do fine but no team that would do it justice, all too heavy, and the ones that would of done was either already reserved for that night or loose on the range. It looked like we was out of luck, and with two nice looking girls on hand to take out.

We tried the only two other stables in Hardpan with no better luck. We couldn't get a driving team nowheres, and we was about to decide on a heavy freight team, for want of better, when of a sudden it came to me, and I liked to scared Grant out of his boots as I jumped up and hollered, "The Blacks . . . ."

As we saddled up and rode out we thought some of the possible consequences with running them in and using them, for horse "borrowing" without the owner's consent wasn't looked at as such in that country then, it was just plain horse stealing, with the thieves seldom being lucky enough to get to jail and trial.

But we didn't worry about that much, for the most important thing with us at the time was to get a good driving team, regardless. Them two blacks was like there to order for us, and about the only thing we was afraid of was if we could find 'em again. Maybe they'd drifted on.

As luck would have it they hadn't. We found 'em only about a mile from where we'd seen 'em the afternoon before, and as we circled 'em and run 'em in, we had no thought of anything but what a pretty team they was and what a showing they'd make. We didn't think as to whether they was even broke, half broke or spoilt buggy wreckers and runaways. All we figured was they'd make a mighty pretty team, a proud one for the girls to be seen driving with.

With some careful maneuvering and sometimes fast riding, we got the team in the stable corrals, and there the stable man had to rub his eyes at the sight of 'em, remarking he'd never seen a prettier and better matched team. "But," he added on, "they act pretty snorty."

Which they was. So, not to bust up the democrat which we figured on using, we went to trying out the team on a bronc cart with heavy wagon wheels and brakes.

After roping the two, they was easy enough harnessed, and we was mighty pleased right then to see that they'd been broke and a sure enough buggy team. We didn't know yet as to what kind, but after we hooked 'em onto the cart without much trouble, then climbed in and started 'em, we was surprised that they acted as well as they looked, which was going some.

I took the lines and drove 'em around the big square feed corral a few times, and being they acted so well, Grant opened the gate and out we went, without a trip or jerk rope on either of 'em. On account of not wanting to be seen driving the "borrowed" team any more than we could help, we took to a lane leading out of town and as we drove along we got to figuring there was no better behaving, prettier and steppers than this team of blacks was. We felt mighty lucky.

After a few miles of driving, we turned back, more satisfied than we ever thought of being with any team. We was pleased some more when, after telling the stable man of their good behaving, he offered to let us use his prized light harness, and as he put it, "the one he'd got married in." The buckles, loops and hames was of brass and all shined up, patent leather with red inlays in some parts, and on that team, hooked to the canopied democrat we'd be fit to parade with the best and outshine 'em.

Noon come and we then went to see Millie and Mazie. They'd be able to come, they smiled, the old cowman had seen the proprietor as to that, and when we described the fine team and rig we had to take 'em along with, they was more than pleased. More so than nowaday's girls would with shiny sports roadsters and marcelled lady killers to drive 'em.

The days being long, the starting time was set for seven that evening, a pretty time of the day to drive. It was late that afternoon when we brushed up the team, slipped the polished brass trimmed harness on 'em and hooked 'em up to the canopied democrat. Then we went to the hotel and slicked ourselves up as much as we could so's to try and match our fancy rig and do credit as escorts to the fair ladies we was to drive out to the doings.

And mighty fair looking ladies they was as they appeared when we drove up to the place of meeting. In shining, rustling taffeta dresses they looked like stepping out of pretty picture books. But as much of an impression as they made on us, that fancy rigged up classy team and canopied democrat we had, made them do some staring too, and as escorts I don't think we looked so bad either, going by their glances.

Stepping out of the rig I helped Millie up to the front seat while Grant helped Mazie up in the back seat, dust covers spread over their dresses and we was all set to go. The sun was shining bright and still over an hour high. It was a mighty pretty evening, long bluish shadows spreading over rough rolling hills and malpais rims, double brightening the natural colors of the land, and all was fine.

I started the team in a good brisk trot and they took to the bit like the good ones they appeared to be, keeping the lines tight and as they should in my hands.

There wasn't much in the way of conversation amongst us four at first but there didn't seem to be no call for any, and even tho I and Grant would of liked to've got some going more free, we didn't know how to go about that very well, and the talk was mostly between him and me, thinking that might start the girls to talking a little too. But I guess our conversation was too much about what we knew only and not enough in common with what they knew and could talk about. There was a sort of tenseness that needed busting.

And a busting it got. . . . We was out of town a few miles and I was holding the two shiny blacks to a fair pace when all at once, and for no reason that I could see, the off horse (the one on the right) let out a squeal, lunged ahead and then sure enough kicked over the traces. Not only over the traces but the tongue too, and then things did start, and start for fair. . . . For the nigh horse (the one on the

47

left) joined in, went to acting up and kicking, and right quick there was a runaway in full swing, with the off horse still riding and kicking over the tongue, a mighty scary and dangerous predicament to be mixed up in, for if the tongue broke and stuck in the ground it would sure up-end the rig to a high and then hard landing crash, to be drug some by the runaway team. Another thing, that country wasn't at all of the kind to enjoy a runaway in. The high, side-winding rocky wagon road around and over steep, rough hills, across deep gullies and arroyos, amongst boulders, tall sage, jack pine and down timber, made me feel that at any time the democrat and all of us would be bounced high and wide to be scattered over the rough, steep scenery.

The rig did go pretty high and weaved mighty scary a few times, and at the speed we was going it was a wonder we stuck. But by then Millie had a strangle hold around my neck and even tho she hollered her fear right by my ear, she sort of steadied me so as I braced myself against the lines and brake.

The runaway had gone on for a fast mile when we come to a fairly steep hill. The road went on sidling and near level around it. But there I slackened on the right line and rode on the left all I could. Millie's weight helped some, and then I poured the whip to the off horse, surprising him out of his wits and drawing his kicking hind leg back off the tongue, at the same time to turning off the road and up the steep hill. It was a good, long steep hill, the sage was tall, and by the time the team got to the top, pulling the democrat with the four of us, and me keeping the brake on all the way up that rough going, they was pretty well winded.

As good luck would have it there was a little flat on top of that hill, and getting there I stayed on and pulled with the left line, leaving the right one slack. That way I kept the team going in a circle, and as they gradually slowed down some, Grant jumped out, intending to grab the off horse's bridle as I circled the team around to bring him and the other to a stop.

With Grant jumping out, that left Mazie to her lonesome, but she didn't stay that way long, for soon as she could get her balance she joined Millie's hold around my neck, from behind, and now I sure had enough ballast on the line, and weight also to steady and hold me, so long as the rig stayed right side up.

By some miracle it did stay right side up, and finally when I got the team more winded in circling and to slowing down some more, Grant got his chance, made a leap at the off horse's bridle and got his hold. Then with one hand closing on the horse's nostrils, cutting off his wind, it wasn't long when they both slowed down to a trot, then to a stop.

The girls let go of their strangle holds around my neck then (it was my first time to be hugged so tight) and they would of fainted after the let down of the scary experience if they'd been of the hot house kind. As it was, and after they'd rallied some they only remarked that it sure had been exciting for a time.

The tenseness on the talk had been busted, and as I started the now quieted team and drove on some more, there was very little holding back in the talk, we'd all got acquainted of a sudden. It'd took a scary ride to do it.

The team went on smooth and at a good pace for a spell and I figured that being they'd now had their fun, they'd go on behaving the rest of the way. Then, as we drove along, I noticed that the off horse begin to lag. He couldn't be tired, I knew, not that tough one,

It was my first time to be hugged so tight.

and then I found out soon enough that he was the real trouble maker of the two.

As he went to lagging more and more I touched him with the whip a little, with no effect, a little harder and still no effect. Then I stung him good, and that sure brought results. But not the kind I expected. . . . He again lunged ahead as before, like to break thru the harness, and once more kicked over the tongue, starting another runaway, as wicked as the first, with the trouble starter kicking over the dash board most every jump.

Instead of being leary this second time I seen red, and when a right opening come I held the end of the left line over to Grant, and while still holding on to it along with the slack right line, I poured the whip to that trouble making black, surprising him plenty more, to forget his kicking, quit riding the tongue and get his long hind leg back to his own side of it.

But they'd sure lined out to run, Millie again hanging on to me and Mazie hanging on to Grant. There was no steep hill handy this time but the low rolling ridges around wasn't bad, only mighty rough riding in the democrat, and steering clear as I could of the deeper washes I kept the blacks circling around and around some more.

There was a scattering of junipers along them ridges which I tried to dodge as I kept 'em circling, then I of a sudden got an idea when the canopy of the democrat near got tore off from over our heads as the team brushed too close to a dry limbed juniper. Then, along with the idea that come to me, I watched my chance and took a long chance when I thought the right time come. A big juniper stood right in the way, and instead of trying to pull the team clear of it, I pulled 'em right straight for it and hollered,

"Hang on everybody. . . ." A second later there was a crash and splintering of cedar limbs as the team hit the tree, each one trying to go on opposite sides of it, with the result that they sure got fooled and stopped mighty sudden. They buckled up like accordions and it seemed like the democrat near done the same as it jammed up against 'em.

Even as braced as I was, I and Millie, who was still hanging on to me for all she was worth, liked to went thru the dash board at the impact, and Grant and Mazie were piled over the front seat, but we managed to stick. The team stood quivering, their heads sticking thru, one on each side of the tree and like they was afraid to move.

Grant jumped out then to see if any of the lines or harness had been broke, but it was all right, and it was a wonder the tongue stood it. It was a mighty good tongue or it would of broke before, when that off horse had kicked over it and layed most of his weight on it as he'd run and kicked at the same time. That was one of his main tricks.

The blacks acted as tho they'd been taken down a peg or two as they was backed away from the tree, and some of the broken branches pulled off their heads, manes and necks.

But I didn't take no pity on 'em, and after I again got 'em on the road I kept 'em rambling right along, sometimes on a high lope and near to runaway speed, just to give them their bellyful of that and sort of keep 'em contented.

The off black seemed afraid to kick over the tongue any more, and being I had pretty good control of 'em I kept 'em rambling at good speed on the winding, rough road. Sometimes the hind wheels of the rig would whip around and scare the girls but they somehow got to having fun at the goings-on, even if they was some leary at times.

We was making mighty good time, driving much faster than I wanted to, for I'd rather have driven slower and enjoyed the company of Millie, and the scenery some. I know we all felt that way but them blacks had other ideas and we pretty well had to go according. Before I knew it we was to within only a few miles of the ranch, down in the valley where there was a few other ranches. Then we come into a lane of fenced-in hay meadows and I slowed the horses to a trot and even to a walk a few times. I figured they was sure all right by now and we all went to talking more free and enjoying each other's company much more than when first leaving town. The two runaway spells had sure broke the ice and we now all laughed and talked about it.

We was doing just that when, only a couple of miles from the ranch and all going fine, all Hades broke loose once more. The off black of a sudden kinked up, kicked over the dash board near up to my nose and away he went, the other right with him on the instant, and on another runaway.

There was no more riding on one line now and pulling the team to circling, for we was in a lane and had to go straight along it. Millie again took her hold on my neck, the same with Mazie on Grant's, and the four of us braced up that way, we prepared to stay, me with one boot on the brake and both arms stretched out on the lines to steady and hold the runaways to the road the best I could. The democrat was bobbing and side-swiping like a can on a dog's tail, and now there was another lane ahead, one that turned into the ranch and there was a gate there.

But as good luck would have it, it had been left open. The main thing now was, could I turn the team into that gate at the speed they was going and be able to hit the opening, keep the democrat from turning over or have it wrapped around the heavy gate post?

It sure looked impossible to make that turn, hit that wide gate opening, which looked mighty narrow right then, and still be able to stay right side up if that sharp turn and gate was made. There was nothing to do but try, for the lane we was speeding on ended right there, at the turn into the other one to the ranch, and so, bracing myself some more and hollering, "Everybody ride," I went to manipulating the lines to make that turn. We all got to one side of the democrat to hold it down, the side that would be apt to tip up at the turn, and when it come time to make that turn, without being able to slow the team down, I handed the end of the left line to Grant and we both sort of "sat down" on it.

That liked to yanked the blacks' heads off, but it done the trick, slowed 'em down for the second it took to make the sharp turn, and even tho the democrat ricoshayed some off the road, it stayed right side up, and on we went, full speed ahead again and straight for the ranch, now only about a quarter of a mile ahead.

That distance was covered in no time, seemed like. Ditch culverts and creek bridges was no sooner saw than crossed over, and to my great relief, when we come to the ranch grounds I see, straight ahead, that the wide gate of the big square corral was wide open. One of the boys at the ranch had seen our dust, and knowing what had happened had rushed over to open that gate.

At the speed the team was going they come near going thru the corral even at that, but not quite, and then we had 'em.

QUITE A CROWD WAS THERE that night, and a great time was had by all, ranchers, cowboys and town folks. A midnight bait of cold meats, cake and much coffee, and the shindig, with fiddles and accordion for music, lasted until daybreak. The girls put their arms around mine and Grant's neck some more, laughing about it, as we danced. It was not the same strangle hold as had been in the democrat. That had sort of broke 'em in to us tho, and we soon seen as the goings-on started, that we didn't need to fear of losing 'em to anyone else for that night.

But we got set back some when morning come, for they said they wouldn't be riding back with us. They went on with how they'd like to and all that but they was afraid, very much afraid every time the team run away. But they added on that they would like to see us again when we got back to town, and that eased us some.

It eased us some more when the old cowman who'd invited us out came and told us that *he* was going to take the girls back himself, grinning while saying that he should of known better than to trust nice girls like them to wild cats like us.

It would of hurt our feelings considerable if they'd been going back with some galivanting shorthorns from town. There was quite a few who'd tried to cut in on us, with no luck. What was more, they'd consented to have us take them to the rodeo on the after-noons of all three days, and that went well, for me and Grant was to contest in some events at that time, and to have somebody in the

crowd to ride for especial, besides the judges, sort of helps some.
. . . We would be right with 'em when no events called us to the
chutes.

Starting from the ranch after that night's doings, the blacks
surprised us by behaving mighty well. But they also had when starting out from town the night before, and we wasn't fooled by their
good behaving. They might bust loose any time, we figured.

Grant drove going back and remarked, laughing, that there'd be
no fair maidens' arms around our necks if the team started running
away now, so there was no use *letting 'em* no more.

I rode in the front seat with him, and in the back seat, to take the
place of the girls, was two of the musicians the old cowman had taken
out of town to play at the dance. That old son of a sea cook had
swapped them on us for the girls, to make room for them in his rig.

Well, we didn't blame the girls any, and we, ourselves, wished
they hadn't been with us a few times the evening before, for fear
they'd get hurt.

But that doggone team now behaved like good ones most all the
way back into town. They spooked only a couple of times, but there
was no kicking over the tongue or real runaway, and even tho the
musicians got pretty scared, we took them in and delivered 'em safe
and sound to where they wanted to go. The sooner the better it was
for them, even if they had to walk some.

Rid of them we drove to the stable, and there we got quite a
surprise for, after we unharnessed the team and turned 'em into the
feed corral, figuring on later taking 'em back to where we found
'em, there come two official looking men towards us and placed us
under arrest, under arrest for horse stealing.

Well that was a great howdedo. . . . The stable man had come near and we looked at him for a sort of help in explaining, about our getting the horses, only to go to the dance and to turn 'em loose again. But we seen there could be no help from him, for he seemed as surprised as we was. He didn't know us nor the horses nor nothing of the goings-on.

According to the officers the two blacks had been taken out of the pasture some few weeks before from an adjoining state. The owner had posted a reward for the capture of the thieves and return of the horses.

We'd been seen driving the team on the outskirts of town and traced to the stable, and there we was.

We went to jail. . . . Sort of stunned, it took us a little time to realize that our chances to compete in the rodeo was all shot, also our meeting up with the girls some more during that time. Neither of us being known but little in that country, having rode for the ⊓ only a few months, there was no chance of getting bail.

It looked bad for us, and being that territory had been sort of overrun with horse thieves that sure didn't help any, and maybe they'd want to make an example of us. . . . But, as there's most always a brighter side to the darkest, we finally come to figure we was lucky we hadn't been caught in the hills with them horses or we might of been up a tree, with a rope around our necks.

Anyway, this was plenty bad as it was, for just borrowing a runaway team of outlaws.

Me and Grant was taking turns pacing up and down the narrow cell between the steel bunks. There wasn't room enough for the two of us to do that at the same time. We done some useless pondering that way and then we'd sit on opposite bunks, look at one another and grin, sort of disgusted like. Neither of us had much to say only maybe to cuss the luck some.

We was taking turns at doing a little of that, and had been cooped up about an hour when one of the officials came to the cell door, talked to us a bit, like sort of to get an inkling as to how we felt, then, thinking he'd be safe, had the jailer unlock the door and let him in with us.

He sat down on the bunk beside Grant, offered us each a cigar, lit one for himself, and pleasant-like asked us to tell our story in appropriating the horses, with that usual warning that whatever we may say might be held against us.

There was, of course, nothing we had to say that could incriminate us and we was glad of the chance to tell our very short story from the start, where we'd been riding, coming to town for the rodeo, the invitation to the dance by the old cowman at his ranch, the girls he'd got for us to take to it, no other team we could get to take 'em, and all the goings-on, runaways, and all till we got back to the stable, when we'd planned to take the team back where we'd found 'em.

The official begin to smile as we told the story and then to laugh at the runaway happenings, with the girls and all. He looked at us different when we got thru with the story, and he looked different to us too, then, not as an official no more.

Then he asked "I suppose you boys can prove you've been riding for the 🜀 until a couple of days or so ago, that you never laid eyes on the blacks until yesterday and drove 'em only to the dance."

"Yes," we said, "by the old cowman who put on the dance. He's well known here."

"I know him well," says the man. . . . He speeded up our heartbeats when he went on with, "I don't need no proof. I believe you boys' story and it might be a good thing I happened in this town as I did, for you might of had to stay cooped up for a few days, missed contesting in the rodeo, and," he grinned, "taking the girls to see it."

"By the way," he says, "I'm the owner of these horses, a doctor by profession, and I just turned them loose because they busted up a rig for me every time I hooked 'em up to one. This is the first time I've known of 'em being driven any distance without making kindling wood of the rig they'd be hooked to, and that gives me new hope, for I have much use for them."

"I think they'll be all right to use now," Grant chips in.

"I hope so," says the M.D., "and besides finding them that's worth very much to me. So I of course am going to give you boys the reward I offered for the finding and return of them."

A short time afterwards we was let out in the sunshine again, with twenty-five dollars more for each of us, extra money to entertain Millie and Mazie with, between events and after each afternoon's contest.

The blacks had given us one big scare, but how things do sometimes happen. . . .

IV

FOR THE SAKE OF FREEDOM

I WAS HEADED FOR WILD horse country. I'd just ended up on a job of breaking a string of fine three and four year old colts for the Kant-Hook ⚡ horse outfit, drawed my money, run in my private horses and was catering to my natural hankering to drift on and see new territory.

I'd often heard tell of a country a few hundred miles to the south, where there was not much else but wild horses and antelope, and some few cattle. It was a desert country, water miles apart, some of the springs was poisonous and many others dried up during summer months. On account of the land being covered with sharp lava and shale rock it was mighty hard on hoofs. Brush feed and scarce grama grass was like on the run, and the few cattle that ranged in that country kept sore-footed and poor by trying to catch up with it, and after a day and a night of rustling for feed, with very little rest in between, they'd hardly get their fill or rest when thirst would force them to hightail to the closest watering place, which would be many miles away.

That was what I'd heard tell of that country, the wild horse country I was heading for. I'd been in many countries like it before and liked 'em well; there was lots of room and no fences and a feller appreciated shade and water more. It wasn't no cow country, and most of the cattle that run in there had just strayed and got to ranging there of their own accord. They'd be rounded up once or twice a year and then left free to range as they wished. It was open country all around and many of 'em would drift back.

But if that perticular country wasn't much fit for cattle the wild horse seemed to do well enough and accumulated there, and being they was on range where there was so few cattle, not many riders come to spoil their peace. Only once in a long while mustang runners would set up a water or blind trap and a few of the wild ones would be caught and shipped out of the territory. But the wild ones kept pretty well up to their numbers, and sometimes, as range horses would join the mustangs, that would help keep the numbers up to about the same, for the range horses would soon get as wild as the mustangs themselves.

The long distances between water and feed didn't bother the wild horses near as much as it did the cattle. They was foaled on hard ground and their hoofs growed to be as hard as the sharp lava rock that covered it. They was near as light on their feet as the antelope that run on that same range and, like the antelope, they'd been crowded out of surrounding countries by wire fences of farms and ranches till they come to that land that was of mighty little use to man for his cattle, and of no use at all for sheep.

Of course that land of the mustang and antelope could be used for the better bred range horse, but the mustang would have to be got rid of first, like has been done in many such places, and so the range horses wouldn't lose their breeding by mixing with the wild ones. The range horse runs as free on the range as the mustang does, only he's used to seeing a rider more often, he won't try very hard to get away, and will turn as the rider wishes or to where he points him, and on into a corral without causing much trouble. In the corral the unbroke range horse is near as wild as the mustang. When first caught he'll fight just as much, and when first rode he'll usually buck harder and longer than the mustang will.

The average range horse originates from the mustang, only he's been bred up as to size for different purposes with imported thoroughbreds and to where he's worth raising and branding. The brand identifies the horse as to who he belongs to, and there's still many branded range horses who show some of the old time mustang blood.

The wild horse goes unbranded, of course. He's just as hard to round up and corral as antelope or deer would be, and if a rider crowds a wild bunch to go to a certain place, that wild bunch will scatter all directions, like a bunch of quail. A strong, hidden corral has to be built to catch them, that's called a blind trap. A water trap is a corral in plain sight and around a spring, one wide gate is sprung on 'em. They'll usually travel a long ways to some other watering place rather than go inside a water trap to drink, for the wild horse is mighty wise, and suspicious of any enclosure.

There's usually no claim on the wild horse, and any man who catches one has got himself a horse free, but there's the catch.

From what's been handed down to me from old-time cowboys who had the same handed down to them from other old-timers before them, and so on, back to the time when the first horses came to America, I get it that them horses was Arabians, and a Spaniard by the name of Cortez brought 'em over by boat from Spain and landed 'em in Old Mexico, where they accumulated and some of 'em got away, run wild and drifted North. Them Arabian horses is the ones our mustangs originated from. They was a wild and sort of inbred bunch but they saved many a man and Indian from walking.

The unbroke range horse is near as wild as the mustang. When first
caught he'll fight just as much, and when first rode he'll usually
buck harder and longer than the mustang will.

What we call mustangs now days has very little of that old mustang breed. That's been mostly bred out of 'em by imported horses, and them that's now running wild are just mixed breeds of range horses that didn't get rounded up regular, and hit for wild country where they seldom see a rider. Like in that wild horse desert country I was headed for. I was two days' ride away from the outfit, where I'd finished up on my job of breaking horses, when I come to a fair-sized cow town. I stayed there a couple of days, got all cleaned up, hair cut and trimmings, supplied up on a pack horse load of grub, clothes and all such as I needed, celebrated a bit and then hit out of town early one morning, headed on for the wild horse country. I had six good horses with me. There was only two I hadn't broke to ride as yet but I used 'em to pack, my grub supply was well tied down on one and the other hadn't been able to buck his pack off either. He was packing my bedding, extra clothes and warbag.

I WAS HAZING MY HORSES THROUGH a lane that led out of town a ways when I noticed two fresh horse tracks along the road, looked like only a couple of hours old on account I could see they was made after the night's dew fall had settled the dust. The fresh stirred earth made by their tracks stood out plain. One of the horse's tracks was of a fair-sized saddle horse, I figured. He was shod. The other horse's track was of a smaller horse and barefooted.

I didn't pay much attention to the two fresh horses' tracks only to glance at 'em, as a feller naturally will. That's a kind of range rider's instinct, to notice all signs and tracks, for stock will stray and the information of such tracks to some owner who might be hunting for them would be helpful to him, sometimes helpful in many other ways. A feller can never tell.

Them horse tracks stayed on the road ahead of me for many miles after leaving the lane that led out of town. I thought at first that the shod horse was being rode, on account of his tracks keeping so straight ahead, but later I seen where he'd sort of checked up to nip at some grass. Then I knowed he was a loose horse, and not wasting much time on his way to wherever him and the barebooted one was headed.

A few miles further on, the tracks branched off the road on a trail that led to some rough hills. I kept my horses on the road which seemed to circle around them same rough hills and sort of forgot about the fresh tracks. But I would have remembered seeing them tracks if any rider had asked me about 'em.

And I did remember them well, for, quite a few days afterwards and about a hundred and fifty miles from where I'd first seen 'em, I run into them very same tracks again and I recognized 'em quick. This time the tracks interested me a heap more. Them two horses sure must be travelling, I thought, for I hadn't wasted no time myself, and they sure must know of one certain range they was hitting for and anxious to get there because, on their trail, they'd had to go through a couple of pretty thickly settled valleys and skirt around or go through one or two towns. Then there was a wide river they had to swim acrost. There was no bridge that I know of to within a hundred miles either way and I crossed my horses on a ferry.

Well, thinking of what places they went through to get to where they wanted to get sure set me to wonder at them two horses, and their tracks got to be more than interesting to me.

BUT IF I WONDERED ABOUT THEM then, I got to wondering about 'em plenty more as I drifted on, for their tracks seemed to be leading right the way I was headed, towards the wild horse territory. From the time I run into their tracks again this second time I run into them some more as I rode on. They was hitting pretty well straight acrost country and taking short cuts on and off trails, where, with me, I'd stick to easier going and sort of circle around the roughest parts. I know that in their cross-country drifting they crossed rimrocked and box canyons where it'd bother a mountain goat to climb in and out of, and as days went on and I run into their tracks now and again I then got to hankering to catch up with 'em and have a good look at 'em. I could see by their tracks and signs that they was seldom very far ahead of me, and sometimes I expected to see them after topping some ridge or mountain pass. I wondered how come they drifted so straight and steady. They seemed to graze and water as they went, seldom stopping, and as they come to bunches of horses, as they did many times, the shod track showed where they didn't stop to mix in and graze a while, as most horses would, but went right on as though they was mighty anxious to get to wherever they was going.

One morning I was camped by the first railroad track I'd seen since leaving the cow town about two hundred and fifty miles to the North. The railroad crossed a river there, and on account of high and solid rimrocks on both sides of the river, there was no way to get down and swim acrost or to get out on the other side. The only way to cross the river right at that place was on the railroad trestle and I sure wasn't going to take no chance of shoving my horses over that, they might get excited and jump in the river below or stick a leg and break it between the timbers of the trestle which was about three or four inches apart and allowed enough space for a hoof to go through.

There was only one way for me to go, that was either up or down the river till I come to a crossing or ferry or wagon bridge, and the going, either up or down that river looked plenty rough.

It was as I was sizing up the hills over my camp fire and by the sun's first rays that I got my first glimpse of the two horses that'd been making tracks ahead of me since I left the cow town. One was a bald-faced, stocking-legged black and the other was a bay filly. They both was good looking horses, specially while I was watching 'em, for they seemed excited as to finding a place to cross the river. They acted like they'd already been up and down it a few times looking for such a place, and when they come down off the hill and to the railroad they stopped, sniffed at the rails and then looked along the trestle, as if they would cross on that.

I was glad that my camp and horses was out of their sight because that might of scared 'em into crossing on the trestle. They trotted on down along the rim of the river and I figured they would find a place to cross down that way. But I'd just about got my outfit ready to pack, put out my fire and was going after my hobbled horses when I seen the two coming back, still on a trot and looking for a place to cross. They come to the railroad, stopped there and sized up the trestle again, more careful this time as if they figured that on the trestle was their only way to cross the river.

They didn't trot away from the trestle this time, they'd just wander a few yards and then come back to it. I watched 'em, feeling a little numb, because I knowed by their actions that they would try to cross that scary trestle.

They came to it once more, the black was in the lead, he lowered his head, snorted at the rails and timbers and made the first few steps on the start across. The filly was close by him.

I'VE WITNESSED SOME HAPPENINGS that caused me to hold my breath but never any for so long a time as while watching them two horses crossing on that high and narrow trestle. I felt chilled and petrified and I don't think I could of moved if I wanted to or kept from watching the two horses. With heads low, bodies crouched and quivering, they snorted as they carefully made every step. One step gone wrong and there'd be a broken leg, or maybe two in the struggle to get free, and then maybe a fall into the swift river a hundred feet below.

As I watched I wished I had scared them away before they started acrost that trestle, but it was too late now. They went on, careful with every step, and as they got near center of the trestle I was afraid they'd get scared at the height, the noise of the river below, the distance they still had to go, and turn to stampede back. That would of been their finish, either by broken legs or falling over the edge. And what if a train come along?

I think I'd given one of my horses right then just to see them two safe acrost the trestle and on solid earth on the other side. But as long as it seemed, it wasn't so very long when they got on the other side, then they let out a loud whistling snort at the spooky trestle they'd just crossed and hightailed it as fast as they could out of sight.

I rode up the river for a couple of days before I found a place to cross it, and as I rode I often wondered at the power of instinct to call a free horse to cross such as the trestle which both was in dead fear of and which no amount of riders could of forced 'em to cross. It was the homing instinct of the wild horse that had called 'em, and I got proof of that some time later.

I'd got to the wild horse country I'd headed for. I'd found most of the scattered springs there had old dilapidated corrals around 'em, water traps. The wild horses had lost their suspicion of 'em and come right inside to water, and figuring on catching a few of them I located a little scope of country, high up where stock wouldn't naturally go and where feed was fairly good for my horses, and there I set up camp, about two miles from the closest spring, and went to work patching up the old corral at that spring so it would hold a bunch of wild ones when I sprung the gate on 'em. It wasn't a regular trap gate, just a swinging gate, but I fixed it so it would swing well, tied a long rope to it so that when pulled it would close the gate fast and tight. I dug me a pit as far as the long rope would reach, covered it up with brush and dirt, leaving only a hole big enough for me to crawl in and out, and I was ready for the wild ones to come.

But I didn't want to use that trap yet. I moved camp to another spring about thirty miles away and fixed another old trap there the same as I did the first, then I came back to the first trap and by that time the signs I'd made in fixing it had been pretty well blown over, and I noticed by tracks that quite a few bunches had come to water there.

MY CAMP SET UP AGAIN, I went to the trap about sundown and got settled in my pit for the night, but no horses came that night nor the next, but the third night was good, a bunch came in. I counted eight head against the skyline and I pulled the gate slambang on the last one's tail as he went in.

The corral held 'em, and the next day I roped and throwed everyone of 'em, tied a front foot to the tail with just enough rope so the foot only touched the ground and was useless for any fast travelling. All the wild ones fixed up that way I went and got my saddle horses, packed up my outfit and brought all down to turn in with the wild ones, and then opened the corral gate and started out.

Being alone I had to do some tall riding to keep all the horses together but the wild ones couldn't get away with a front foot being held back, and when about four or five miles from the trap, they finally settled down to follow my saddle horses.

On account of the mustangs having one foot tied up I could only drive 'em about fifteen miles the first day. There was no water in that distance and the horses was thirsty, so I changed saddle horses and rode all night as I let the horses graze and drift on slow. It was high noon the next day when I come to a spring and there I cooked myself a bait and let the horses rest close to water the whole afternoon. When night come and it got cooler I started 'em on the move again, found water late the next day and in a corral close by I took the foot ropes off the mustangs. They was well "herd-broke"

The wild ones couldn't get away with a front foot being held back.

by then. That is, they would turn the way I wanted 'em and stay in one bunch, with my saddle horses.

I'd drove the horses about six days from the time I left the trap when I come to a big settled valley. In a lane leading to the town I met a rider who helped me drive the horses to the shipping yards on the outskirts of the two, and I sold 'em there the next day for eight dollars a head, a fair price for mustangs in that country.

My saddle horses rested up some, I headed back to the wild horse country. I used the second trap this time. Mustangs get suspicious quick if one trap is used often. I caught only a small bunch, six head, but being I had no way of keeping 'em till I caught another bunch, I took 'em in. They was all grown stuff and brought me ten dollars ahead.

I think I caught and took in three more bunches after that. I remember there was fourteen head in one of the bunches I took in.

Fall was coming on, but the wild horse country was still hot and dry and I wanted to catch another bunch before a rain come, leaving plenty of water everywhere and making my traps useless.

I was at one of my traps early one evening. The sun hadn't gone down yet and I was enjoying a smoke by the shade of the corral when I seen two wild ones coming. I could tell they was thirsty because they was coming on a trot. I didn't want to bother with catching only two, but I didn't want to keep them from drinking, and I crawled into my pit without first investigating if rattlers or tarantulers had crawled in there, as they sometimes would.

The horses, always suspicious of a water trap, even if it hasn't been used for years, slowed up when they come to within a few hundred yards of it and snorted and sniffed as they carefully came closer. It was then that I recognized the two horses. They was the two that had trailed ahead of me for over four hundred miles from the North. They was now on their home range and the reason I hadn't seen 'em before is that they'd been watering at other places in the wild horse country.

As I said before, I didn't want to bother with catching only two horses, and when them two came in the trap, and after they'd drank some, I somehow couldn't help but slam the gate closed on 'em. They was surprised, of course, as the gate slammed and they tore around some, but they soon quieted down again, and with a sort of hopeless look came to a standstill. They'd been caught before and they seemed to realize mighty well that their freedom was lost once again.

I got out of the pit and climbed into the corral. They only stood and quivered and snorted, and as I watched 'em I noticed that the black horse had wore his shoes off, but he had a little spot on his back that would never wear off, that was a saddle mark.

As usual when inside the trap I had my rope in my hand, and to get better acquainted with the black horse I made a loop and flipped it over his head. As I'd already figured long before, he was a broke horse and he didn't try to break away when I caught him. Instead he turned and faced me and only snorted a little as I pulled on the rope and led him up to me. He was gentle, and whoever had broke him had not broke his spirit. He was still the wild horse at heart, and if free again in his home range he now was in, he'd be harder to catch than the other wild ones which had never been caught. He'd be wiser and harder to get into traps. It was nothing against his wisdom that he'd been caught in my trap because it was old and sure looked desolated.

The black was far better built than the average wild horse in that country. He was good size too, and I judged him to be only about six years old. A good horse, and I figured I could sell him for near as much as I could get for any ten head of average wild ones I could catch there. The filly was good too, but fillies don't count much in the wild horse country.

I decided to keep the two horses. I went to where I'd hid my saddled horse in the brush and rode to my camp where I crawled into my regular bed. Night had come but I didn't go to sleep for a long time, I got to thinking of the two horses in the trap, and as I did it came to me how much their freedom and home range meant to them. They'd run away from a country of plenty grass, shade and water, where they'd been well taken care of. Their condition proved that. Then they'd drifted acrost rough countries, through lanes and settlements every wild horse fears, swam rivers and even crossed on that scary trestle, all to get back to a desert and barren dry country. But that was their range, and wild freedom was there.

I thought again and again of their crossing that strange and spooky railroad trestle to get to that home range of theirs, and now, after only a short while of freedom they was in a trap again, and I'd closed the gate on 'em. I'd took away the freedom they'd risked so much to get back to.

The stars blinked down at me. I set up and rolled me a smoke and, still thinking of the two horses in the trap, it struck me kind of queer when it come to me of a sudden that there was nothing to stop me from opening that trap gate and giving the horses their freedom again. That thought seemed to relieve me a considerable. I finished my cigarette and then went right to sleep, all peaceful.

Who'd ever heard of a wild horse hunter turning horses loose after he'd caught 'em. Such a thing is never thought of. As I rode down to the trap I got to thinking as I did the night before that a couple of horses more or less sure wouldn't make much difference to me, and whatever money they'd bring wouldn't mean so much either, not near as much as the pleasure of seeing them go free.

Besides, I had plenty enough money. I didn't need no new saddle and the rest of my outfit was good for plenty more wear, then I had a string of mighty good saddle horses and there was thousands of miles of range country. What more could a cowboy want?

But I was kind of cheated in the pleasure of carrying out my plans, for as I got to the trap I seen it was empty. Them two daggone horses had found a hole in the trap, they'd made it bigger and squeezed through.

Well, I thought, it was a good thing they got away because I might of changed my mind. I looked down the big desert flat and couldn't even see their dust nowhere. I grinned as I thought how wise they was and how hard they'd be to trap again.

I patched the hole in the trap, figuring on catching one more bunch of wild ones before leaving that country. For I was again hankering for new range. I stayed in the pit two nights. No horses came, then big clouds piled up fast during the third afternoon, seemed like from nowhere, and I hardly felt the first few raindrops when whole sheets of it came, soaking me through.

It seldom rained in that desert, but when it did that time it didn't come down by drops but more by bucketfuls. In a short time every little dry wash was a roaring river, boulders was washed away like grains of sand, and from the high knoll I'd rode up onto I seen my trap washed away like it was made of toothpicks.

The cloudburst didn't last long, only about an hour, but it had sure moved a lot of country in that time. It was like big dams had broke loose from everywhere at once, and the big hardpan flats which was sizzling hot a few hours before was now transformed into big lakes. Plenty of water for the wild ones now, I thought, and they wouldn't be coming to water traps to drink for some weeks. By then more rain would most likely come, for winter wasn't far away.

The country sure looked clean and fresh and smelled good as the sun came up the next morning. It gave me the good feeling to ramble on over it, and as I boiled my coffee I got to thinking of another country I'd heard tell of and which I'd never seen. It was located some few hundred miles further on south, and as winter was coming on I figured the mild climate wouldn't go bad, for a spell anyway.

V

CHAPO—THE FAKER

F EW SADDLE HORSES ARE the size Chapo was. The name Chapo didn't at all fit him and maybe that was why he was called such. For Chapo is Spanish for a small, chunky horse and this Chapo was everything but that. He wasn't only tall but broad and weighed close to thirteen hundred pounds, the weight of a good size draft horse. But he carried that weight mighty well, was proportioned and built about perfect, and he had the quick fast action of a nine-hundred-pound cowhorse.

Mighty few saddle horses of his size are much good for fast and hard range work. Such horses are used mostly for corral work, snubbing or heavy roping, or "riding bog" (pulling out bogged down cattle). But when such a size horse is a good one, meaning in action and what all the smaller horse is, he's usually a *very* good one, as good as he's rare.

Chapo was one of that rare kind. With all his size he was active as a cat. He was very much that way when I come to work for the outfit he belonged to and was turned in my string. But he was of no more use by then, even tho he was still of good age, fat as a seal and had never been hurt.

He'd turned tricky, and fact was, as the foreman frankly told me, he hadn't been rode for a couple of years on that account. That was all the foreman told me about the horse, which is considerable more than a cowboy is usually told about any horse when he hires out to any outfit. If he's told, especially by the other riders, he won't listen, for he's apt to be told just the opposite of how this or that horse might act. That's done partly in a joking way but more to test the newcomer as to his experience—if he's a top hand, medium or of no account, if he's rode far and wide, is a home guard or just green.

That's usually guessed pretty close soon as the new hand catches the first horse in his string. A string ranges from six to sometimes as many as fourteen head of different kinds of horses for different uses, to each rider, and the cowboy who's rode far and wide, for big outfits and is a good hand doesn't ask about any horse in the string that's turned over to him, nor listens to what he might be told about 'em. With his experience in handling more than many and all kinds of horses, he practically can tell the caliber of most any horse by a glance of him and the second his loop tightens around that horse's neck. If not then, he'll usually find out at the first sitting.

But some horses, not going the humans one better, don't show their true caliber until some particular thing happens. That might not show up until after a dozen rides, and when you might get to think you know and can trust him, he'll bust wide open with all the meanness that's really in him, catch you napping (unawares) and get you, all depends on your sense of riding and general knowing of horses.

It would of been as well for me, or maybe better, if that foreman hadn't told me about Chapo being tricky. I didn't ask him in which way, but just the looks, actions and great size of that horse was enough to warn any cowboy who dabbed his rope on him.

He stopped sudden, turned and faced me quick as my loop settled over his head, and holding it high he followed my lead, snorting, out of the bunch. Well, I figured right there, he sure wasn't a jerk-away anyhow, and that was one fine point, especially when a rider is off his horse and many miles away from camp.

With his head held high the way he did, he looked as tall as a giraffe and my five feet eleven more like that of a pigmy. But for a horse that hadn't been rode for a couple of years, and fat and good feeling as he was, I didn't think he was so bad, just acting natural. It was also natural when he struck at me a couple of times as I come up the rope to within touching distance of his nose. I was expecting that, and to put an end to such action I flipped the end of my rope around his front feet. I seen then too, the way he just stood and trembled, that that had been done to him plenty times before and well busted (thrown) when he run against it.

Watching his hind hoofs, which might reach up quicker than I could see, I then put my twisted rawhide hobbles on his front ones. The next was to slip my hackamore on his sky-high head, and there's where I had the beginning of some trouble, for he was mighty headshy and would hardly let me touch it. But by going easy I managed to work a half hitch over his nose and I could then touch him up to his eyes. I got the hackamore that far, and there I was stuck, for he held his head not only near out of my reach but jerked it as I'd try to get the hackamore headstall over his eye and close to his ears, and as he'd jerk that way he'd rear and strike with both hobbled front feet. But I'd be close to his shoulder at such times and the flying hoofs would graze past.

I seen then, as I tried to ease the hackamore headstall over his eyes on up, that he had a "bug in his ear." Sometimes such head and ear shyness *is* caused by a bug, maybe a wood tick that gets in the ear and makes a sore. But with Chapo I could see it was only plain fear of being eared down, which I found out afterwards had often been done so'd he wouldn't kick the rider while getting on or off of him.

After his two years of freedom he was of course much touchier about that left ear of his, and no matter how easy and careful I tried, I couldn't get my hackamore above his eye. But I'd had dealings with such horses before, so, instead of trying to slip the hackamore from the front and over his eyes up to his ears, I unfastened the headstall, slipped it around his neck to the back of his ears, where I wanted it, and fastened it there. He didn't seem to mind that so much, and being that on a horse broke to the bit I also used a bridle over the hackamore, I slipped it on his head in the same way.

Bridling was about the worst about him while handling him from the ground, and by easy stages I gradually broke him of that, for I didn't twist his ear to get on or off of him, even tho at different times I come near having to do it.

He wasn't so bad to saddle, not if he was hobbled and you didn't jab him in any way the while. When such happened he could bring up a hind hoof and kick well ahead of his shoulder point, from a standstill and even tho hobbled. As I've already said he was active and limber as a cat.

I figured I was sure due for a tough ride the first time I prepared to get on him. It's always best to expect the worst and be ready, but what I was leary of the most was them far-reaching hind hoofs of his as I'd go to get on, that that would be one of his tricks.

Without taking the hobbles off and standing well by and ahead of his shoulder, I took a hold of the "bosal" (hackamore nose band)

and bridle cheek with my left hand. Chapo stood a-quiver at that, like ready and expecting me to reach for the stirrup. I felt that, and so, instead of reaching for the stirrup with my right hand, I reached for the saddle horn, wiggled the saddle some to make sure it was on tight enough to stay, and then, to the tense horse's surprise, I of a sudden doubled up with both knees to land high on his shoulder, to ride alongside there and just ahead of the saddle.

Well. . . . That horse liked to've had a cat fit at that trick, which I seen right away had never been tried on him before. I was too high for him to reach with a hoof, and as he went up in a wide-winding buck-jump, being hobbled and out of kilter, he near doubled up on his neck instead of landing on his feet as he came down, and I, being free, easy cleared his fall.

I was again on his shoulder before he got entirely to his feet but he didn't do much high flying jumps any more after that, just circled sideways some and tried to whirl me off. . . . When he finally come to a standstill and while all a-puzzled, I slid down to the ground, took off the hobbles and then eased into the saddle without him hardly seeming to realize. Anyhow he didn't make a move.

And when I did move him, and sort of made him come to with a light pop of my quirt, it was my turn to be surprised, for instead of lighting into the powerful and hard bucking as his actions all indicated he was sure aching to do, he just went to crowhopping, then to bucking, but not hard enough to throw even a stool-riding drugstore cowboy off.

I must of looked my surprise, for a few of the riders that was near had to laugh, and I was then told that that was about the worst bucking he ever done.

That horse like to've had a cat fit at that trick.

I rode Chapo when his turn come, every two or three days, and thought he was a good circle horse (for round-up rides). The tricks I'd so far found in him wasn't any worse than could be expected from most circle horses, for them are horses that can't very well be used as cowhorses. They're usually the kind that take no interest in the ways of handling stock, and it's up to the cowboy riding 'em to put 'em to work in covering the country, rounding up and driving whatever stock is found to gather all in one herd at the "cutting grounds" (where what stock is wanted is held and the not wanted cut out; that's cowhorse work).

The circle horse string is usually made up of mature colts, cold-jawed and spoilt horses. Tough ones, and it don't matter so much if they can't be turned on a dime, as the good cowhorse can do, so long as they can stand a good ride at good speed, and can be turned to within a hundred yards more or less while chasing and rounding up stock.

After riding Chapo for about a month, whenever his turn come, I got to figure that the worst of his tricks was when I handled him from the ground. I finally cured him of them pretty well, but according to what the foreman had told me of him I kept a-thinking there sure must of been more and worse tricks than the ones I'd found to make the foreman pass that remark and warning. I had other and worse horses in my string than Chapo was and nothing was said of them. So I kept a-thinking there must be some other and still worse tricks in him which hadn't as yet come to the top or he sure wouldn't been left to run loose for two whole years. Not on account of what few tricks I had discovered in him.

I wouldn't of course ask the foreman as to what trick or tricks he meant Chapo had, for, as range etiquette points out, it's not the proper thing to do. So, as I'd be riding him once in a while I'd be wondering, and sort of curious as to what hidden tricks Chapo might have deep in him, which he'd be apt to bust out with most any time. That made me keep alert and sort of tense and ready for when one would pop, and that's where I felt it would of been better if the foreman hadn't warned me of Chapo's trickiness. I figured I could of been a match to any of 'em.

But as it was, always on the watch out as I ro bde him, he sometimes got me to do some scary wondering. Like for instance, when riding him on the top or steep side of a high peak that horse seemed to sense that I was anything but bold and brave when up so high in such places. Maybe he felt it by the way I hugged my saddle so tight and was so much nicer to him away up there.

There come one especial time, while I was riding him amongst steep pinnacles, high razor-back ridges and narrow ledges, when that horse kept a-spooking and gave me about all the scares I could stand for a spell. This was in a badland strip of country, deep ravines and near bottomless holes. But there was some pretty fair feed took hold in crags and amongst the little brush in some places. The wilder cattle would hit for such country during round-up time and hide away in there. Consequences was, that rough country had to be rode much closer than the more open.

I think I rode my saddle closer than I did the country that time, for Chapo seemed to enjoy scaring the life out of me by acting up at the most dangerous places, like spooking at his own tail, even saddle strings, and other things he wouldn't spook at any other time. He'd then hump up, jump around some and like he would go into a bucking or stampeding fit, right in such places where even a mountain goat would be careful of every step and the missing of one would mean a downward trip to China.

I somehow managed to live thru the scares, combed my scope of what cattle there was in it, and them being plenty fat and wild they didn't need chasing when once found out. They just left that country at the sight of me and as tho it was haunted, and the echo of my holler, when I wasn't too scared to, worked as if spooks was on their tails.

My circle done and finally getting out of the badlands to catch up with what cattle I'd scared out and thrown with more bunches other riders had got out, the scares that Chapo horse had given me begin to sort of react on me, against him, for now that the most dangerous places was past he was as well behaving and willing as he'd been spooky, ornery and stubborn before.

That made me peeved to the point where, as I thought on his scary tricks, I finally got good and mad at him and decided to take all the orneriness out of him right there and then, also whatever other streaks of trickiness he might have away deep in him. I was seeing red, but I gave him his head so he'd be free to bring on all the action he wanted and all to his heart's content as I hooked him in the shoulder and unlimbered my quirt on him.

The first jump he made liked to broke my back. But I'd asked for that battle, and at it we went. I'm sure that, according to what the boys had told me, that Chapo bucked very much harder then than he ever had before. He done a sure enough powerful job of it and I wished some of the boys had been near to see for I knew they'd agree with me. I was high and wide from my saddle quite a few times during the battle, and I wasn't mad no more now as I kept dragging my quirt on him all I could, I was just determined, determined to whip all that orneriness out of him and whatever more he'd been storing, and to win that battle, I had to.

And I did, even if it was nip and tuck a few times . . . he finally throwed his head up and broke into a crowhopping run I was glad of it, for I'd had about enough too.

It was a couple of days later when it again come his turn to be rode, seldom over half a day to the turn, for we changed to fresh horses three times a day. He was snorty as ever before when I caught him, like he'd forgot all about the battle we'd had and of his losing it.

I knew his caliber and that what ornery streak was in him could never be taken out. He'd have that in him for as long as he lived and was able to navigate. But what still stumped me was what trick or tricks was it that the foreman remarked of that horse having. It sure must be odd and special ones, and which hadn't showed up as yet. I'd sure given him all the chances and encouragement to bring out all the bad that was in him, and even tho he'd turned on most every trick and twist a horse could the last time I'd rode him, there'd been nothing much out of the ordinary from what all a good tough and ornery horse would do. So, by that and the foreman's remark I figured there must be still more to come.

Thru curiosity I come near asking him, but again thinking the better of it I decided to forget about it and take that horse as he come. Him and me had only that one battle and after that we got along well, as well as could be expected.

Then, a short time afterwards, when it was again his turn to be rode I noticed as I caught him that there was a sort of halfway meek

I was high and wide from my saddle quite a few times during the battle.

look in his usually watchful and challenging eye. He was also some easier to bridle and saddle. I got on him without feeling I had to watch for a hind hoof, and when I started him out for that morning's ride he went along like a good one.

Even the other riders noticed that difference in him, and there was grinning remarks such as, "Maybe he ain't feeling well," or, "I guess it's a change of heart," and so on passed around.

The last remark, the one about a change of heart kind of stuck to me. Maybe, I thought, the ornery son of a wolf did decide to change to the good, maybe a long pondered on conclusion from the good battle we had. Then, I thought again, or was it that he'd pondered on the other trick or tricks of his which the foreman had remarked about. . . . Maybe he was scheming on that now, to catch me napping.

But he wouldn't catch me napping, I figured, or getting too careless. . . . Nothing happened, only, when just a few miles from camp, I thought I felt him favoring his left front leg. A ways further on I was sure of a limp in that leg, and then, a couple of miles more and that horse was sure enough lame. . . . Too lame to go on and it would be plenty hard enough to get him back to camp I thought, so as to unsaddle and turn him loose.

That lameness all come on him before we got to a point where the foreman would scatter us riders to different points, to circle and comb the country of what stock was there, driving all to the round-up grounds, near camp.

As we rode along, I noticed the foreman looking at my limping horse and sort of grinning to himself. I wondered about that, also that he didn't seem at all concerned about the horse's lameness. But

I was, and was about to tell him I'd be turning back when he beat me to it, and grinning some more, he just said, " All right, Bill. We'll see you in camp at noon."

It then came to me as I turned Chapo back for camp that there was something queer about his kind of sudden lameness, without a run, twist or jump to cause it. Then the foreman's knowing grin. . . .

It came to me all the plainer as, a ways after I'd turned the horse towards camp, he begin to lose his lameness, until before I got there it was practically gone. I knew then what was up. That wise Chapo had faked that lameness, and when he was again turned loose with the remuda (saddle bunch) there wasn't a sign of a limp in him.

I'd had horses fake in different ways with me before, but none had acted the part quite as well as Chapo had, and another thing, whether Chapo had been faking or not there's sure no pleasure in riding a lame horse. There was many others, and mighty, mighty few ever fake.

That noon, during the change of horses and as I caught another horse, the foreman told me that now Chapo would play lame for some time, maybe until round-up was over, then hide out on some other range when time for the next round-up come.

He was a wise one. If he couldn't outdo his rider, and one got the better of him after all his tricks had played out, he'd always fall back on the one trick such as the one he'd played on me and finally won. That was his hole card and the trick I'd wondered about. Fake lameness.

VI
THE TWO GHOSTS

"H EY, SAM! DOES YOU-ALL see what I sees?"

The shaky, like-unbelieving sound of the voice made the one spoken to turn to look at the speaker who, with an out-stretched arm was pointing off to a distance.

Sam looked that direction and then his voice also got shaky and like unbelieving. His eyes bulged as he finally spoke.

"Why, Lige," he says, trembling, as he stood up, "Is them horses I sees, or ghosts?"

"It ain't all so much what they might be," says Lige, not at all reassured by Sam's tone of voice, "it's what they's doin'."

Sam's eyes bulged out some more as he then noticed. "Why, it's bones they's chewin' on," he says, shaking in his boots. "L-l-o-o-ks like one of 'em is a-gnawin' on the skeleton of a man's hand."

The two very nervous observers got close together at that, to better discuss what they didn't want to believe they was seeing, and as the discussion went on there was two listeners, who squatted on the ground nearby, begin to perk up their ears at the thought of the possibility from what all was being said in the discussing. A possibility that tickled their funny bone.

The two listeners was only two of the twelve or more cowboys that was scattered here and there and all around the round-up fire.

It was twilight, the round-up boss was still out, with a few more riders and to bed down the herd for the night.

This was a cow camp of the southern desert ranges. Sam was a colored boy of about thirty who'd just drifted in from Texas and got a job with this outfit as nighthawk (herding the saddle horses at night), and Lige, some older than Sam, was also a colored boy and hired to cook for the round-up camp. He was a fair cook but with what little time we got to know him in we seen he was much better at driving the four-mule chuck wagon when moving camp than he was at cooking.

As to the subject and reason for them two colored boys' discussing that evening, the cause was the appearance of two old white saddle horses which we called The Ghosts. Their names was Pete and Blanco. Blanco was one of those rare white-borns.

The two being so old had been pensioned for many years and before their usefulness had gone. Being the good cowhorses they'd been they'd many times earned their freedom, also care when they needed it.

But they hadn't needed no care, and far as their freedom was concerned they had that, but they didn't hit out for the wild bunch so as to enjoy it. Instead, and after so many years at following the round-up works they still tagged along from camp to camp over that outfit's range, like the two old-timers they was, mixing in with the younger ones that was throwed in the "remuda" (saddle bunch) every year and as tho' to keep in contact with what all had been their life's work.

Them two old pensioners was never driven along with the remuda from one camp site to another. They was left behind to follow and graze along as they wished. They'd most always be left where the last camp had been, and there to eat up some of the scraps the riders would clean their plates of after each meal, such as pieces of biscuits, potatoes, meat, rice and what all goes to make up a cowboy's meal. When all of that, with some extras left a-purpose, was cleaned up, the old horses would then slowly drift on the way the outfit had gone and towards the next camp site. They knew the location of them all very well.

It would seldom take the wagons and remuda over half a day to move to the next camp site, some longer for the herd. But with the two old pensioners having a lot of time they seldom would reach it until about sundown, often during the night. They'd sometimes come into camp while we'd be eating and bum us for biscuits or such like, which didn't go well with neither the cook nor the foreman, and when it'd storm and cold winds blowed they'd put their rump against the chuck wagon box for shelter, or if the outfit or any of the boys had the luxury of a tent, that was still better to back up against, but sometimes they'd back up too hard and there'd be howls from the tenants inside.

It was Lige and Sam's first sight of them two old white horses as they drifted in close to camp that evening. The colored boys had been with the outfit only a couple of days and hadn't noticed 'em before. For that reason the quiet appearance of them two ghostly looking horses all by themselves more than made up for effect.

That effect and the colored boys' actions is what first drawed mine and Soapy's attention towards them. We was the two riders that was squatted near where they was standing at the time, and at a nudge in the ribs from Soapy, the rider beside me, I knew that some

If the outfit or any of the boys had the luxury of a tent, that was still better to back up against.

ghostly idea had come to his mind. When he later whispered it to me I found I had near the same.

It was a fine twilight and background for such ghostly ideas as what had come to us. The sky to the east was near black with heavy clouds, and with the reflection of the sunken sun and twilight from a clear sky to the west shining on the two white horses against such dark background, they sure did show up more like ghosts than any earthly animals. Especially to the two superstitious inclined colored boys. We seen by their expressions and excitement that they figured for sure the two old white horses was ghosts, and with their mind going wild that way it would look as if one of the horses was sure enough chewing on the skeleton of a human hand, when in reality it was only a few jointed, sawed-off ribs of a beef which the cook, whose place Lige had taken, had throwed away a few days before.

The two old horses enjoyed chewing on bones about as much as some youngsters do on hard candy, and that evening they seemed to be enjoying that all the more and was making a great show of that, like for the benefit of the colored boys who by then looked on as tho hypnotized and petrified, neither able to say a word. To add on, the other white horse then picked up a long shank bone which we figured would sure look like a human leg bone to the numbed colored boys. They couldn't give no comment as to that and at the sight of 'em, Soapy nudged me again, and grinning to look like the very devil himself, he stood up, quietly got close behind the two fear-paralyzed boys and with a weird, rasping voice slowly begin to speak.

Their feet couldn't seem to function and they didn't twitch a muscle or turn to look at him as he begin, ghostlylike, but by the flickering light of the fire it was plain to see what went on back of their shining, bulging eyes.

"Them spirits you see," Soapy was saying, in a haunting tone, "are of the departed. The horses have died of thirst many, many years ago after their masters was brutally murdered, and every night since then their spirits come to eat their masters' bones and take their spirits with them. It's not bones nor horses you're seeing, it's the spirits of them all and as it happened many and many long years ago—"

Soapy might of went on some more, but happening to glance my way to get an idea on how he was doing, and then at the other riders around, who all by then was looking up and wondering what the samhill he was up to, he didn't trust himself to say any more. He seen that if he did the jig would sure be up and all the fun spoiled.

So, leaving things be as they was, and careful of not making any sound, he came back and squatted by me again, without the colored boys seeming to realize it was Soapy's earthly voice that'd come to their ears. And as a fine ending, like made to order for the ghost story, the two old white horses slowly turned, and heads down went and disappeared in the darkness.

Sam didn't care to do his nighthawking alone that night. It was near a mile to where the remuda of over a hundred saddle horses was to be herded to graze, at the mouth of a malpais-rimmed canyon, and Lige, being the cook, with no horses for his use, walked alongside of Sam to where he would be holding the horses. He didn't want to be away from Sam that night either.

All that kept the two boys from hitting out that night or at dawn the very next day was that, as the foreman had said, the outfit would be moving camp in the morning. Then they figured they would be out of the ghosts' territory.

Soapy and me had a hunch as to what they'd figured, and when the next day come and we all went to riding the surrounding country for what stock was wanted, us two branched out from the other riders and rode on, maybe a little beyond the country we was to cover that day but it was to an aim with the scheme we had, for the benefit of the two colored boys.

With the cowboy, being out in the hills and riding hard most all the year around, about the only enjoyment there is what's made up from every chance that comes along. Some maybe rough and scary but none with any intent to harm anybody, nor just of the plain foolish kind either. There's got to be a good sense of humor to it even if the victim doesn't see it for the time, or is being punished or showed up for something or other. The victims usually try to even up, but the plotters are seldom found out and that's what sort of keeps the ball a-rolling for amusement in cow camps.

The stirring up the two white horses brought on the colored boys was too good to let pass without more being done about it, and that was with Soapy's and my scheme that we rode on further that day. It was to get the ingredient necessary to carry on that scheme, that luminous stuff called phosphorus.

We knew a prospector who used that chemical in different ways with his work in minerals and diggings, and we figured if we got a little of the stuff we could do wonders with what we had in mind.

We found the prospector working at his diggings, got a little of the phosphorus from him and we rode on back, taking what cattle we found and drove 'em on in to the round-up grounds. Considering the extra riding, we got there not much later than the last bunch before us, near to another camp site some miles from the one of the night before, and as we rode in to eat and change horses, we had to grin at one another as we noticed the colored boys' relieved and contented actions, for they'd got away from the ghost spirits of the horses, murdered men and haunted territory, they thought. Now we hoped the two white old ponies didn't disappoint us by not following or showing up that evening, for it would be a good dark night and just right for what all we planned.

They didn't disappoint us. They showed up just right, before it got too dark and to put the colored boys into another huddle of fear, and then disappeared again as they had the night before.

The effect on the boys was much worse than that of the night before, for now the spectres was following to haunt 'em, and they figured there'd be no getting away from 'em wherever they went.

Soapy didn't add on any weird talking to the spell that evening, for two good reasons, one that he couldn't of controlled his voice for laughing, and the other that if he could, he was afraid they would hit out in a mad run and quit the country, spoiling what more there was to come. Beside, we had to get busy.

Seeing that the two would be sure together on nighthawk again, like with misery fear loves company, we went on with our plans. We had plenty of time to put 'em thru and enjoy 'em, for there was about six hours before our shift on nightguard (with the cattle herd) come.

As the talk died some with the fire, and the riders, one by one, begin to hit for their bed roll scattered here and there amongst the sage, we went to our own rolls, took off our spurs so as not to make any sound, grabbed a couple of cold biscuits we'd hid, and with short ropes went on to catch the two ghost horses.

Being so used to coming into our camps and getting biscuits and such came to a good advantage then, and by right maneuvering we easy enough caught 'em, gave 'em their biscuits, and then led 'em on to where we'd piled up some bleached bones which Soapy and me had gathered earlier that evening.

The bones was ribs from scattered old carcasses of cattle, and them we figured would play a good part in our program, as the rattling of skeletons. We tied a few of the longest ones to the horses' manes and the others, bracelet-like, around the ankles to clatter on the gravelly earth as they'd travel.

That sound, along with the apparition of the two white horses would of scared any superstitious person, not mentioning the two already primed colored boys.

But we wasn't thru yet, the phosphorus still had to do the big part, and using a sage twig for a brush we proceeded to paint stripes as to outline the ribs and whole skeleton of each horse with the luminous paint.

That was a job which took us quite a spell, but with the fun we was having at the thought of what the results would be near made the job a labor of love, and by the time we got thru and looked over our masterpieces we seen where we could easy have got scared ourselves if we hadn't been the creators of such work. We even wondered at the horses not being scared of each other.

All that seemed like going to a lot of trouble at the time, considering what little fun we might get out of it but we didn't think of that right then, and before that night was over we was more than satisfied and repaid for the planning and trouble we went to. Yes, much more, and in many more ways than we expected.

Very much satisfied with our work we then started on leading the two ghost horses for where Sam and Lige would be, somewhere near the remuda and most likely popeyed with watching all around.

Wanting to get close enough to them before being discovered so we'd get full benefit of their actions, we got near to one outside edge of the remuda, hid our two horses and waited for them nighthawks to make a round of the grazing remuda.

A light breeze was blowing, sounding like a moan thru the scrub brush, and with the dark of the cloudy skies, that all went well for our purpose. We couldn't be seen in that darkness but the luminous ribs and skeleton painted on our ghost horses glowed a sickly greenish yellow and looked mighty scary.

We sort of fidgeted while we waited, but soon enough we heard the faint sound of a tune being whistled, then the same being hummed and we noticed there was considerable nervousness to both the whistling and the humming, such as might sometimes be heard from some one going thru graveyards during dark nights.

The tune, or chant, kept a-coming closer, we crouched to the ground, and when we finally outlined the two darker shadows walking alongside of each other, one leading a horse and now only a few paces from us, we freed our two horses, got behind 'em and slowly started 'em the direction of the other horses of the remuda. The luminous skeletons and rattling of bones would pass a few feet in front of Sam and Lige and we crawled along behind our ghost horses close as we dared to see the results.

The results was mighty fleeting. There was a deadlike pause of the two figures for a second or so, like maybe they was petrified with fear, then sudden unearthly hollers, cracking of brush twigs, and more hollers and cracking of brush as they went, or flew. They must of flew, for it was but a very short time when the repeated hollers sounded far distant and then couldn't be heard no more. Our scheme had been a success.

And what a success. So much so that we didn't hardly have time to laugh at the goings on, not until the hollers died out, and then it was sort of short-lived, for with all the hollering they'd hit for the remuda, then the two old white horses also hit that direction and right on the flying colored boys' heels. The ghost horses was now playing their part too well.

At the apparition of them, and with the colored boys yelling like comanches, all hitting for the center of the grazing remuda, the scare spread like lightning thru all the horses, and away they also all went into a stampede, the ghost horses right after 'em, for they'd also got scared by then, in wondering what the other horses got scared of, and natural-like wanted to get in with 'em and stampede too.

With the rumbling of running hoofs we of course knew what had happened and now our plans for a good joke and laugh had turned to much concern. We forgot about Sam and Lige for the time, figuring they'd soon enough stop running and circle back to camp. The remuda was the main thing now, and being we was the cause of stampeding it, even tho not at all meaning to, it was up to us to head them horses off and bring 'em back. We knew that Sam and Lige, in their fear, couldn't be bothered with any horses right then.

We of course sure had to get our saddled horses to be able to gather up the scattered remuda, and not wanting to cause any suspicion, we'd left them at camp, which was about a mile away.

The ghost horses was now playing their part too well.

Neither Soapy nor me was very good walkers at our best, but that night we ambled along in a dogtrot and covered the distance to camp in pretty fair time, for us. When we got there, near out of breath, we was surprised at the commotion. All the riders was up and some already riding away on a high lope. We'd got there just in time to join 'em for we knew the herd had stampeded then, and we soon learned that it was on account of the remuda stampeding into it. The few bell horses in the remuda would be enough to cause the stampede, but thinking of the two bone-rattling ghost horses along with it, that would be enough to stampede anything, even some of the cowboys.

We got on our night horses and rode hell-bent for election, with all ears for the sound of the running herd and bells of the remuda. Soapy and me wasn't talking nor thinking of the recent joke right then, for it'd got beyond that and the results out of control. Our ghost horses was maybe having the time of their lives but they was carrying things too far.

It was too dark to see any distance ahead of us, but Soapy and me managed to stick together and soon enough we heard the rumbling of hoofs, then darker masses a-skimming over the brush. It was cattle. We rode close to the herd, or a part of it which had split from the main one, and as we turned 'em our ears was more for bells of the remuda than that of the herd, for the ghost horses would be with some part of the remuda and they was the ones we was after. They'd sure be easy enough to see.

We stuck to that bunch of cattle until we run onto other riders with another bunch, then turning that bunch over to them we went on to looking for another bunch, a bunch of horses, mostly, and with the two ghosts tagging along. There was no asking any of the riders we passed or near bumped into about them ghost horses, for every cowboy was riding fit to kill, some as tho they'd sure enough seen ghosts.

After turning a couple more bunches of cattle we finally heard bells, bells of the remuda, but these horses was just part of it, and being the ghosts wasn't in that bunch and it wasn't running much no more, we just turned 'em and went on looking for a bunch with the ghosts in it.

From the time we started on with the stampede we must of rode steady and at good speed thru the pitchdark night for a couple of hours. The other riders had of course been at it the same, and the way the herd and remuda was scattered, it would be an all night's riding for all of us and most of the next day until all stock was gathered and accounted for. There was over a thousand cattle in that herd.

But that same night and after a couple of hours of hard riding we finally did run onto our two ghost horses. They was by themselves, like they run out of stock to stampede away, or maybe they'd just got tired. Anyway, it took our horses quite a spell to quiet down at the first sight of 'em and then we had to ride on the windward side so they would get a good whiff of 'em to make sure that the two ghostly looking objects was after all sure enough horses.

Having had a good run we had no trouble roping the two old ghosts. No biscuits would done then, besides we had no biscuits.

Feeling lucky of catching them before they spooked the stock to any more rampage, we started leading them away, making a roundabout circle so's not to run into any more stock or riders.

Our intentions was to lead them to a creek a good distance away and there wash off the luminous stuff which had stirred such a commotion with the stock and routine in general.

We was doing fine and riding along a shallow dry wash when going around a sharp turn in the wash a rider looms up sudden and near bumped into us.

He would have bumped into us if it hadn't been for the ghost horses we was leading, for at the sudden sight of them his horse liked to went thru himself in turning the other way.

But we was caught with the goods. There was no use for us to run, and thinking it was only one of the riders, we'd let him in on the joke and maybe get as much laugh about it as we first did.

He did get a laugh out of it but there wasn't the tone to it we expected. We rode on, took care of washing the luminous paint off the two horses, turned 'em loose then rode back to help the other riders with the gathering of the herd and remuda as well as we could during the dark of the night.

Most of the remuda was gathered, and as daylight finally come, many of us rode in to camp for some breakfast and a change of horses. Being the nighthawk was missing, we drove the remuda on in ourselves, leaving a few other riders to hold what there was left of the herd, to be relieved soon as we had our breakfast and change of horses.

But when we got to camp there was no fire there as there should be long before that time of the morning, no steaming black coffee pot, hot skillets nor ovens with hot grub and all waiting for us. It was like a deserted and dead camp, and there was no answer when the foreman hollered at the country around for Lige, the cook. He'd sure disappeared nobody knew where.

Maybe he'd show up. In the meantime there was plenty of work to be done, so we all pitched in and fixed up a hurry breakfast, and it was about over when the foreman remarked.

"It's queer that the nighthawk, Sam, has disappeared too. The horse he was riding with his saddle still on him is in the remuda. Him and Lige must of hit out together."

He was quiet for a spell, the while, squinting under his hatbrim at Soapy and me, then he went on.

"I wonder if them two old white pensioners that was fixed up as ghosts didn't have something to do with the disappearance of them two colored boys, also the stampeding of the remuda and then the cattle."

There was no comment from any of the riders around, then the foreman went some more. "I've seen two of you boys leading them ghost horses and I know which two of you it was. I also am sure it was no intentions of neither of you to stampede the stock, but you did, with wanting a little fun with Sam and Lige, and now that they're both gone it's up to you two to take their places until another cook and nighthawk comes along."

"The rest of you boys let's go and gather up the scattered stock and all watch for signs as to which way Sam and Lige went." The foreman grinned a little. "Sam must of went in some hurry to've had no use for his horse."

Soapy and me didn't move as the other boys got up and left. We just squatted where we was, looking sort of sheepish and neither saying a word. We'd had our joke and now we had to pay for it. It had boomeranged on us and even tho our new jobs was anything but to our liking there was no quitting now. Like living up to a lost bet.

Sam and Lige never did show up again, never nowheres near that outfit's territory. But as they went on to working for other places we'd often hear rumors of 'em and how our outfit was sure a devilish haunted one, and that no God-fearing creature should ever enter its borders.

VII

MONTE AND THE JACK

I WAS TRAVELLING LIGHT, on a good strong horse that could eat up miles with the same ease as a good skiff flanked by a right breeze skims over the seas. I wasn't leading no pack horse to hinder in the travel, for I was going a long ways, to visit with a friend acrost the Border for a spell.

Being the distance I had to cover was such a long one I wasn't hitting it on a high lope, for, wanting to make sure of getting there and saving my horse's strength, I kept him at a running walk or jog (slow trot).

Monte, as I'd named the horse, was holding up fine, picketing him when in the grasslands or hobbling him in the brush country whenever I stopped him for rest and to feed, never in any of the few towns that was passed on the way. There was no set time or distance for the day's travel. When it was cool I'd travel during the day, stopping for a couple of hours during high noon, and when it was hot, which it generally was at that time of the year, the travelling was done mostly at night or before dawn of mornings and away after dark of evenings, spending most of the day by whatever shade could be found.

Over half the distance to where I was headed for was passed when, after covering a long stretch without water, and coming to a trail which in that country always led to a spring, (this was in the

111

heart of the desert) I rode and followed the trail along a desert range and finally came onto a good spring late that night.

Monte was some tired after that long, hot and dry ride and I hated the thought of hobbling him, but I sure also hated the thought of being left afoot in *that* country, and being that Monte was such a restless horse, even when tired or with other horses, always wanting to drift, I wasn't going to take any chances with him.

After giving him plenty of time to slowly drink his fill, I led him up the steep and rocky mountainside a few hundred yards above the spring and there, seeing there was a good scattering of bunch grass, where he'd have to move but little to get his fill of the strong feed, I not only hobbled but side-lined him. Sidelining is tying one front foot to the hind one so they're about three feet apart and the horse can't hop along as he might with only the front feet hobbled.

Monte was well used to that, and being the kind of a horse he was, he'd sometimes cover good distances with all the foot ropes, where most other horses would hardly move more than a few yards around. He'd even often lay down, hobbled and sidelined that way. Something which few horses ever try.

So, him being so wise and not seeming to mind the hobbles, and after seeing the good feed for him that evening, I didn't feel so bad about hobbling and side-lining him then. He'd sure get his fill and I'd also feel sure of having him when day come.

When day did come I rolled out of the hole in the ground where I'd kept my hip all night, looked across the wide stretch of desert then back and up the mountainside to where I'd hobbled Monte that night. There was nothing of him to be seen, but being there was considerable Juniper and such along there, he could be close and easy be hid from view.

I et some of my soda crackers, cheese, and jerky, which was all the variety I ever took when travelling light, for a good quantity of that, enough to keep a feller going for many days, is light and not so easy tired of. There was, of course, always a little salt for when some wild meat could be got . . . . I never packed a canteen, not even in our dryest of desert. It only makes you thirstier in the long run, keeps a-hammering as you ride, and besides, I figure if your horse can stand the thirst you also can. If he can't you're no worse off than he is. You then don't know the desert nor how to save your horse, and you don't belong in nor on either.

After my spare breakfast, enough water to make up for the day, I started up the mountainside towards where I'd hobbled Monte and tracked him to where he might of drifted from there.

A horse, especially if hobbled, will most always graze uphill. More so in rocky desert hills, for the higher up the better the feed. If there is any it'll be up there, while from the springs on down the big desert flats it's usually long miles before any is found. But loose range stock are likely to always drift back the easier going towards the flats after tanking up on the water at the foothill springs. That's much on account of the desert stock being more or less sore footed and with a bred-in instinct to be saving of 'em, for the trails back to the flats are beaten to soft dust for miles to the scattered grasses and eatable brush, while the sharp lava or granite rocks on the steep hillsides above the springs don't seem to hardly draw but few stock, even tho the feed is better and stronger amongst them rocks, and very much closer.

That makes it very good for the rider who comes along with one or more horses and makes camp near such springs, whether he's riding on that range or just drifting thru, for after watering his horses good and then taking 'em well up the steep, rocky sides of the hill to hobble them, one, or two or all, or maybe only the leaders, he's pretty safe of them not drifting for at least twelve hours or so, or until they want water again.

After knowing the desert as I figured I did and how not to lose a horse there, which I never as yet had, I felt pretty sure that Monte wouldn't be far from where I'd so well hobbled him that night, in good feed, and after being well watered and all, some tired too.

So, it got to be surprising to me as I went up to where I'd left him, up ledge after ledge to where I could get a good look for a good distance around, farther than I figured he would or could go, and didn't see hair nor hide of him nowhere near where he should of been.

I jumped down from the high ledges then and went back to, trailing him, from where I'd left off to have my first look around.

I trailed him a short ways as he'd zig-zagged to grazing, with no sign by his tracks that he'd intended drifting. Then I come to where the tracks was all mixed with the ones of another. The gravelly earth had been stirred, as if there'd been a fight.

And there sure must of been a fight, for as I followed the scattered and then bunch tracks of Monte's shod hoofs and that other's long, narrow, unshod ones, I come onto a shredded piece of rope. It was a piece of Monte's side-line rope. A ways farther, amongst more fighting track signs, I seen more shreds of a soft rope. This was from the hobble, and now Monte was footloose. Not a thing was holding him.

As I suspected, and soon seen, his tracks was sure far apart and made fast time from there on, down off the rocky mountainside

And there sure must have been a fight.

and on for the wide stretch of open desert. I could see there'd been a chase and that Monte was in the lead, for when the long, narrow tracks wasn't alongside of his, they was on top, and like sure chasing him on.

I knew what kind of animal would make such as the long, narrow tracks but I didn't know there was any of that murderous kind in that country. The tracks showed plain there sure enough was, and as I followed Monte's down towards the edge of the open desert, where I come into more narrow tracks along with that of many horses, all headed for the open country, Monte's tracks mixed in with 'em.

I didn't stop to think I was sure enough afoot; as I trailed back up to the spring I very well knew I was. I seen where the bunch of horses and mules Monte was now with had watered at the spring that night. The stud jack, supreme chief and boss of the bunch had got wind of Monte up above and as is with them lantern-jawed creathures had went to him with true intentions to kill him. Monte breaking his hobbles and then being faster than the jack was all I figured might of saved him. But I wasn't sure about that, for even tho he'd run on with the bunch, a jugular vein might of been cut, for him to bleed to death later on, away out in the big desert stretch where the bunch must of roamed.

I knew the jack wouldn't allow Monte or any other gelding or stud to run with or even come near his bunch of jinnies (she burros) and mares. But Monte, I knew, was the kind that liked to aggravate and, if still able, he could and would outrun and duck that mean jackass to a fare-ye-well and trail along, even if only to be aggravating him and just drifting with the bunch.

116

Being I couldn't ease my feelings on that thick-jawed jack's hide and not having a durn thing to do for the time, I walked on up to the higher ledges again, for a better view of the land below, and thinking that maybe I'd get to see the bunch in the wide stretch below or maybe Monte. But Monte was a gray and he'd been hard to see in that land of the same color, even if he'd been to within a couple of miles. And in that wide stretch where a man could see for fifteen miles, a bunch half that far and the dust of one the full distance, there wasn't any of either come to my sight.

It would of been not only foolish but very useless to've tried to track down Monte, for, even if I'd caught up to him, and whether he'd be with the bunch or not, he wouldn't of let me come near enough to him to put a rope around his neck. He would never let me while he was out of a corral and foot-loose, not even if I had a bucket of grain in my hand to coax him, for he was no pet.

My only and best bet, I figured as I sort of limped back to where my saddle was and squatted by it, was to "hold camp" (stay where I was) until that bunch with Monte, or Monte by himself, came back to the spring to water again.

I didn't mention it before but there was a juniper corral around that spring. The spring came out of the edge inside of it and the overflow sunk in the dry gravelly earth before it got out. It was a regular water trap, with a gate that sprung closed by the pull of a wire from a man who is hid down in a covered pit at a distance.

There was no horse round-ups in that country. The horses and mules was as wild as mustangs, run in very scattering bunches over a powerful big territory. It would of taken a lot of hard riding to've rounded up a few of the bunches, and caused a lot of sore footedness and loss of flesh. And so, water traps was built at each far-apart spring and the riding consisted of going from one spring to another, to wait some days at each until bunch after bunch came in to water, then spring the trap gate closed on 'em. When it was figured the stock watering to a spring was checked up and attended to, the riders moved on to another spring to do the same.

The rounds of the traps was made once or twice a year, colts branded and all salable horses or mules, with one front foot tied up to their tail so they couldn't run, taken to one main camp and pasture where all gathered was brought in and then driven on to market.

The trap corral at this spring was in fair shape, looked like it hadn't been used since the year before, and with a little fixing would easy enough hold a bunch. I went to work on it a little, propping up a post here and there, patching with juniper limbs and tying up the strips of rawhide that was wrapped around from one post to another and which had broken in places.

The sun got high and hot. My boots got to smoking, for practically new, only got 'em about a week before, and with the high spike heel on 'em they wasn't at all for any manual labor, but to fit a stirrup only, and the pointed heel for a sure foothold while handling horses on the ground and bracing against a rope while afoot. Their purpose is as important as calks or spikes are with different games' shoes, and of not much use for anything else.

Back to my saddle again, I took on another spare meal of my very limited grub pile. I seen where I had only enough for about three days, if I made my meals far enough apart, and small enough. There was no game in that country, nothing but plenty of lizards and side-winders. "Sand eels" (snakes) are good eating but I didn't want to think of getting to the stage of having to eat any. I'd figured on reaching a place I knew where I could stock up with plenty to go on, and if it hadn't been for being set afoot by that ornery jack I would easy made it, but. . . .

After a make-believe good meal of crackers and cheese I chewed on bits of jerky, took a little siesta in the shade of a juniper and then spent the rest of the afternoon finishing fixing up the corral the best I could and to seeing that the gate worked good. The pit had to be dug out and recovered over some, then the trap was all set.

There was no moon but the skies was clear as with my saddle blanket to lay onto I crawled into the pit for my night watch. I went to drowsing some but my senses was alert and, by the stars, it was about midnight when I heard the light sound of hoofs and low sniffing snorts of a bunch, always suspicious, coming, and finally go on into the trap.

I let 'em drink, for I knew they'd of course be mighty thirsty and it would be quite a little time before they'd have their fill and start coming out again.

Peeking out thru the cover of my pit I could see the dark shapes of about twelve head in the bunch. My eyes used to the darkness, I could easy tell that my gray, Monte, wasn't in that bunch. But maybe there was one that I could make use of, to riding and looking for Monte, or only to take away the dread feeling of being afoot that would help some. I never was used to being afoot.

When the bunch seemed to've about had their fill of water and some started to nose their way out, I raised up on my pit, pulled on the wire and in the wink of an eye had the gate closed to latch on 'em.

There was quite a commotion at that, and the corral was tested pretty well as the bunch lunged against it in surprise and fright. . . . I waited till they quieted down some. Then, as they stood, bunched and quivering, I eased my way into the corral, rope in hand, to get a closer look at 'em.

I soon seen that none was worth my pulling the gate onto, not for my use. They was all mares and mule colts, and one big dangerous-looking jack which I'd like to've tied down and pounded the ears off of, just to ease my feelings against another of his homely breed for being the cause of setting me afoot, and on other general principles.

But that wouldn't of got me nowhere, besides there might be another bunch coming along with one among it that would be fit to use, maybe with Monte in it. So I opened the gate and let that bunch go, making the gate ready for another bunch.

I went back into my pit and took catnaps until along near daybreak, when another bunch come. It was about the same kind as the first, all excepting one, one that might of done in a pinch but I wasn't feeling that pinched. That one was a filly, looked like about three or four years old, and trim built, wild as an antelope and of the kind that would only fight to a finish, the finish being a wore-out horse that nothing could be done with, not able to take another step, and I'd be left much worse than I already was, for I'd again be afoot, miles from water, and my saddle would have to be left there, with me to hoof it back as best I could. . . . I would of taken a chance on an outlaw gelding or a stallion, but with such as a rattle-brained filly she'd have to be handled and rode some close to camp for some time, many days, before she might be of any use. Even then, she'd be apt to keep herself wore out fighting until she couldn't stand much of a ride, no matter how kind or patiently she might of been treated. . . . So I decided to let her go.

Come sunup and no more bunches showed, not even a far-away dust telling of any to within miles. But I had hopes that Monte might of been kicked out of the bunch he'd started out with and come to water during the day, if he was still able and in the surrounding country. Him not being wild, he wouldn't wait till night to come to water if he was alone and thirsty. But if he was with a bunch such as them who roamed that country, I wouldn't expect him to come until that following night, for them desert-bred horses and mules usually came to water only every other night. Then again, I got to thinking, they didn't always water at the same spring, and so, if he was with any bunch he might not show up again for a week or even much longer and be watering at some other springs, whether he was with another bunch or alone. There was no telling. . . . But there was still hopes, especially for that night.

No bunches came in that day, it was a long hot one. I went up the mountainside some, amongst pinons and crags and places where I thought I might scare up a cottontail or a sage chicken, for I was thinking of my dwindling grub supply and as the case is when such runs low, a feller seems to get all the hungrier. But that wasn't no game country of any kind and all seen was lizards and side-winding rattlers. There was plenty signs of mountain lions, too.

That night was a very disappointing one, for, expecting Monte then more than any other time, all that come was one bunch of about the same kind as the two of the night before and I just let it go again. Monte might of started out with one of the different bunches

I'd caught but I of course had no way of knowing, whether he'd had to leave it and went on, or what. Anyway it looked like he, alone or with a bunch had sure left to water at some other springs to return I didn't know when, if ever.

Being no other bunch come that night I had to make the best of it and wait until the next night, still hoping against hope that Monte would show up by then. But that would have to be my limit of sitting and waiting, for, by then, what little grub I had left would be gone and I'd sure enough be facing starvation . . . unless I killed one of the mule colts, which, according to mountain lion's taste, is much better eating than horse, and again, much more so than a good yearling calf.

But that wasn't thought of, only as safety against a case to where if a man would have to cut on his saddle or boot tops for the makings of a stew in order to keep from starving. I was still far from that stage.

After a long, hot and restless day the third night come, and with the cool of the evening my hopes revived some. I wouldn't be afoot when morning come, I felt, not if I had to ride one of them thick-jawed and thick-skinned jacks. With a good shelalay which I'd whittle out of the scrub-oak bushes around, I could keep his roman nose off my leg and his homely head bent the direction I'd want him to go.

I got into my pit, and as night wore on till away near daybreak I got to thinking I'd have an even bigger disappointment than I had the night before, for it didn't look as tho any bunch would come that night, none at all, and I got to now wishing I'd kept that filly of a couple of nights before. She might of turned out better than I'd figured, and feeling sort of hopeless about that time, I got to thinking

122

she might of turned out to be right good. I could of kept her for one day anyhow, I thought, in case nothing better turned up, and tried her out.

I was cussing myself some for letting her go when I heard the faint hoofbeats of a bunch lightly snorting their way in, and at that sound I stopped breathing for a spell, listening to make sure. And sure it was a bunch coming but mighty slow, careful, suspicious and spooky-like. They'd come to near entering the trap, then of a sudden turn tail and run back a ways, to turn again and were ready to jump in a split second at not even a suspicious sound.

They came near the trap a couple of times that way only to run back, and finally, being nothing happened, the smell of water won 'em, and into the trap they went.

I didn't wait for them to drink as that bunch got into the trap this time. I sprung the gate on 'em as the last one got in and I had 'em. They would have plenty of time to drink, for I wanted to keep 'em in the corral until daylight, when I could look them over good. I only took a look to see if Monte was in it. He wasn't, but if he happened to come alone or with another bunch, I'd let this bunch go so he could come in. In the meantime I sure was going to hold one of this bunch I had for I had to ramble to where I could get some food before I run out of notches in my belt and would have to wrap it around me twice.

I must of snoozed some, for it was sunup before I knew it. I crawled out of my pit, went to the corral to get a look at the bunch in the bright sunlight, and "lo and behold," as the feller says, there was that filly that'd come in a couple of nights before, the one I wished I'd kept, and with the same bunch. It was no wonder they'd been so spooky coming into the trap again that night, after the other night's scary experience of having the gate sprung on 'em. But it was a big wonder they come to that spring so soon again, instead of going to another.

But I didn't ponder on that long. I hitched up my belt so I wouldn't eat what little I had left in one gulp, then, with my rope and hackamore, I eased into the corral. The bunch run and snorted around me as I got to the center to look 'em over well again and make sure which one of the bunch might do best. The jack was too old, and battered up from many fights, none of the mares or mule colts would do, none but the filly. She was of the right size for good saddle stock, built for speed, strength and endurance, and rolling fat. And, to my big surprise I seen that, as she turned from one side to the other in going around the corral, there was no brand on her. All the others was branded close, even to the yearlings, and the filly was at least three.

Well, that meant a couple of things. The people of that country was either mighty careless with their stock, or truthful, or was sure death on horse thieves, or that filly would sure be branded. . . . I couldn't ponder long on that point either, and seeing she was my only bet I had to take that chance. Even at that I wasn't taking as many chances as I would of with a branded animal, for I'd near have to bump into the owner or some who knew her before there'd be any argument. Then again, I thought, maybe she was a decoy to catch a horse thief with.

But decoy or no decoy I was hungry, would soon be much hungrier, and would have to have something to ride and get some food while I still had strength, or butcher one of them mule colts, which

124

would of been much worse but not as dangerous as borrowing a horse unbeknown for a spell.

I shook them thoughts as I shook out my loop and dabbed it on that filly's front feet, throwed and tied her down. Then I opened the gate, let all the others go and closed it tight again.

There was no use of taking any time trying to gentle the filly or teach her anything as to answer to the pull of the rein, one way or another. That would take a whole lot more time than I had right then, and if I rushed her she'd only wear herself out and get nowheres. I had to get somewhere, and if I could haze her that direction with my hat I would get there, or closer to there, much sooner than if I dillieddallied around with her.

I slipped my hackamore on her head, a small piece of rope thru her mouth to tie around the bosal (nose piece) like for a bit, and with my mecate (hair rope) for reins that would work well on her uneducated head.

I also saddled her while she was down and by the time I got thru with that she'd sort of quit fighting the footrope that held her tied. The filly was round and fat and I worked hard to get the saddle so I figured it would stay, for there'd be no getting off her for a spell because, not being hackamore broke, she might jerk away from me.

Considering all, it didn't take me long to have her saddled, all set, and ready to go. . . . I then opened the corral gate, for I didn't want her to waste any time or energy inside of it. I wanted that for the outside and to make distance.

After another one of her struggles against the foot-rope and knowing she'd figured she was tied down to stay and would lay still for at least a minute or so I took the footropes off without hardly her knowing it, coiled it on my saddle, then crawled into as much of it as I could my own self.

I tapped her on the neck a few times to get her up. She went to struggling then, like she was still tied, but being there was no more rope on her feet she got up with a lunge, I got full seat and other stirrup of my saddle at the same time, and before that lunge could turn to be the start of a bucking spell I scared that out of her with my hat and some other scary motions so that she didn't want to stop to buck. She wanted to get away, and that she sure did, me a riding.

Downcountry we went, straight for the big stretch of desert, and there's where I wanted her to go, out of the rough hills and junipers to open country where I figured I could handle and turn her easier, without taking chances of being brushed off by trees, or have her fall down steep hills or washes, for she was sure stampeding, blind, didn't care where she went and there was no controlling or handling of her, not as yet.

I tried to slow her down a few times so's to save her strength but she'd only fight her head, go to bucking and to running on again as hard as before. I was also afraid she'd fall when she'd go to fighting her head, so I let her run on, checking her as much as I dared and at the same time try to turn her the direction I wanted her to go, that was to the right and parallel to the range of mountains we'd left.

As she got a little winded and slowed down some I finally eased her to go that direction. It was hot and her being so fat she was pretty well lathered up but she kept a wanting to lope along at good speed, not caring much which way she went. I didn't want to try and check her too much because by then my saddle was getting too loose

Being there was no more rope on her feet she got up with a lunge.

for safety and one twisting buck would start it to turn to her side then under her belly, leaving me to reach for the earth, and afoot.

The saddle got so loose that I finally had to do something before I lost it and the filly too. I had a sack tied to the back of it which I used to pack my little amount of food in. It was now empty, so I untied it, brought it forward, slit it on one side, and as the filly was showing signs of getting tired and was down to a slow, dragging lope, I didn't think there was much buck left in her, and so, taking it easy I slipped the sack over her head until it well covered her eyes to a blindfold.

She was soon stopped after that. Then I slipped out of the saddle and right away had her hobbled so she couldn't get away from me. Then I fastened the blind so she couldn't shake it off to see and I looked to my saddle. It was sure time that I did and it was only by my juggling it that it had stayed on her back.

It being so hot I pulled it off so's to keep her back from getting scalded. Being blindfolded and hobbled she hardly moved as I did. She was pretty well winded and breathing hard, and now that she had no chance to get away I let her rest for a good two hours while I chewed on the last of my jerky which I had in my shap pocket, and then smoked cigarette after cigarette. Something I didn't have much chance to do since leaving the corral, some twenty miles back.

We'd gone quite a bit out of our way but that sure couldn't be helped and it was a wonder at the filly's stampeding that we did so well and she stood the pace so long. With the-out-of-the-way wild ride I was still only about a third of the way to where I wanted to go. That was back the way I come, to a railroad water tank which I'd passed by on my way down. Most trains and all freights stopped there to water and I figured on catching one, to go back to another range where I'd left a few saddle horses. They was on good range of an outfit where I knew they'd be safe. I'd decided to leave them there until I got back from my visit acrost the Border. I would of had no need of 'em, for there was plenty more down there. But the losing of Monte sure forced me to change my plans to go on that way.

The filly, now all the sweat dry, and sort of rested up, was again some frisky as I slipped my saddle back on her, but the blind and hobbles quieted her so she wasn't hard to saddle and I cinched it on to stay this time.

I took off the hobbles, slipped into the saddle, and as I pulled off the blind she wanted to stay in one spot and buck, so I had to spook it out of her again and she lit into running some more, but not in the blind stampeding way as she had at the corral. I had her headed the direction I wanted her to go from the start this time, and without having her fight her head at the pull of the hackamore rein I held her down some and to save her strength as much as I possibly could.

But she'd given about everything she had in her first and too fast a burst. She was now tiring out fast, and when them kind do, their spell over with, they sure do mighty quick, for they seldom go on their nerve, but will sulk instead and just quit.

I was sure afraid of that, for the country ahead sure still looked mighty big and a long distance to the water tank which I still couldn't see. It was beyond a faraway rise from the mountain range.

But the filly wasn't at all worried about my getting there. She'd had her wild spurt and now she was ready to quit. After a few miles her dragging lope slowed to a trot, then an aimless walk and a stop.

There's no use of whipping such a kind to make 'em go on for they don't know what it's all about, for what reason or what's wanted of 'em, not when they're confused and just taken from their wild freedom, as she'd been. Whipping her at such a time would only made her sulk to the point where she'd wear herself out all the more and not even feel the lashes.

The best thing to do in such a case is unsaddle and turn 'em loose, till they come out of it, if you're at the home corrals, but that wasn't my lucky fix. So, I done the next best thing, got off and unsaddled her again. I didn't bother to even put the blindfold on her this time. She just stood, like in a trance. But I did slip the hobbles on her and kept hold of my long mecate, for such kind sure come out of them trances mighty sudden sometimes, like out of a bad dream, and sure go to acting up.

While squatting on the desert earth, smoking, and with only my hat for shade I went to thinking, of not my predicament, which wasn't so bad, but of the filly. She'd done better than I expected she would, and now, if I was to leave her where she was and make the rest of my way on foot, which I could of done, even tho painful, she would surely die, die of lockjaw. For she'd stand where she was, until maybe the next day. It would be another day before she'd slowly drift back to her range and still later, to the spring for water. By then, with the sweating she'd had, overheated of her own wild accord, that would be the cause of her getting the lockjaw (the jaw muscles contracting to draw tight so no water, much less food, could be taken).

Thinking of that and realizing that it was very doubtful of her making it back to water in time if I left her where she was, made me scrutinize the hills only a few miles away; I knew desert hills and could sometimes tell by the lay of 'em for near as far as I could see them if any water would be there.

The close hills I was scrutinizing looked promising as with my eyes I followed a lead of 'em to one spot. If I could get the filly to that spot I was pretty sure of finding water for her there. If not, she wouldn't be any worse off than where she was.

After a couple of hours of squatting and smoking I stood up. The filly showed new life and some of the wild sparkle came back to her eye as I did. So, I had to cover 'em with the blindfold again before saddling her. But she behaved pretty fair as I lined her out again and I had hopes that she'd make it to the spot I'd located even if it was most all uphill to it.

A couple of stops had to be made but I finally got her to the spot where I figured would be water. There was. That is there was damp sand after I dug by a ledge and below a patch of rye grass and couple of willow stems. There was juniper up there, and with a dry limb of one to loosen the sand and then scooping it out with my hands, I managed in time to make quite a hole, all the while seeing it wasn't to be labor lost. For as I dug down to where my hands couldn't reach no further there was real moisture and water begin to ooze in. A couple of hours afterwards, and just before sundown, there was about four inches of water in the bottom of the hole, and more coming right along.

Being the filly was now dry of sweat, cooled off and wouldn't be sweated up no more, a few swallows of water now would do as well to ward off all danger of lockjaw as if she drank her fill. Reaching down the hole with my hat I scooped the crown of it full of fairly clear water by hand. I then blindfolded the filly, for the sight of a hat held up to her nose sure would of been sort of scary to her. But not seeing it and even tho the water being held up to her nostrils and mouth was some scary surprise at first, I didn't have to make but a few tries before she, after a sip or two, took a few swallows. Then I had her and she took about three hat-crownfuls before I got thru with her. She hadn't been thirsty as yet but she would have been, and after the sweating she'd had is when the lockjaw would of got her, before she would of tried to get to water.

I took a few swallows of the water myself. Then, as the sun went down and it got cool, I saddled up the filly again, figuring that she could now go quite a ways or maybe all the way to the water tank. But the wild runs she'd made had been too much for her all at once. It would take her a day or so to get over that, and so, after a few more miles, and seeing she wouldn't go much further, under any kind of treatment, I rode her to a tall pinion where I unsaddled and turned her free, without having turned a hair (sweated) on her and so, with taking her time getting back to her range and water she'd be without danger of lockjaw. Good desert feed to browse on along the way, and soon again she'd be the same wild, spirited filly she ever was, only a little the wiser. She'd turned out as a fine saddle animal for anyone who care for mares as such.

I watched her slowly start back for her range, far as I could see her in the darkness, and then, by the light of the stars I hoisted my saddle as far up the tall pinon tree as was necessary so it was well hid from any passing rider amongst the thick and heavy needled branches, then making sure of its location so I could easy find it again I hit out, afoot, acrost the remaining distance to the water tank and railroad, where from there I was to ride a smoke-belching, one-eyed iron horse.

I guess I still had about eight or ten miles to go to reach the water tank and railroad, but I was sure sprung into action and made record time covering that distance, for about a couple of miles from the pinon where I'd hung my saddle I near stepped on the buzzer of a side-winder. I of course left the earth sudden, only to land to where there was a couple more such buzzers right close.

Not being able to see them in the dark I jumped from there too. I was kept jumping and hitting at a high pace from there on for it seemed like there was a buzzing or buzzings every few yards or so. I sure must of got in the home grounds or a den of 'em, and, to make it worse, it was at that time of the year when they're blind, along about August, when they're most dangerous and strike at the least sound. Then the ground being warm from the day's heat, they hadn't crawled into any holes or cracks and was very active, as active as a side-winder sure can be.

I skipped and hopped and jumped at the all-around buzzing for a good couple of miles or more, and then, after that dwindled some and finally quit, I still was spooky and kept on at a mighty good gait. There was the very likely chance of coming onto a few scattering ones most any place in that country, and every brush twig catching or scraping along my boot tops or brushing along a rattle weed, kept me at a mighty fast jumping pace.

Boots might be a good protection but fangs go thru them too. Anyway I sure didn't linger and just stroll along at ease. I went, and the boots being new, still tight, and the heels being high, didn't hinder me none at all. I think I done near as good time and record as most any sprinter, high or broad jumper ever did right then.

I think I done near as good time and record as most any sprinter,
high or broad jumper ever did right then.

By the stars I could tell it was still before midnight when I reached the railroad and tank. I think I made mighty good time, for a man who for many years hadn't walked any further than from bunk house to corrals.

I was pretty warm from the so unusual speed I'd put on covering the distance, and I hit for under the water tank where, with holding my hatbrim under a dripping leak, I got all the water I wanted to ease my thirst. Then, being the shack of the tank man was dark and I was now more tired than hungry, I stretched out on the sand to the east side of the shack, so the early morning sun would get at me soon as it rose. For I'd get chilly and the warm rays would be very welcome by then.

I didn't want to wake up the man to get in the house, for I was in no mood for talking and I knew that my coming at that time of the night would arouse curiosity, and questions would be asked. That would of been too big a price for even a meal and coffee which would of sure went well right then.

I must of relaxed and needed rest bad, for I barely heard the going by of a couple of trains during the night, and it seemed like I no more than hit the ground when the warmth of the sun and buzzing blowflies woke me up. Soon enough there was a stirring in the shack, and not waiting to be caught napping like a tramp, I got up, brushed myself as best I could and walked around to the door.

The door was open and as my shadow came across it, a mighty surprised man of about thirty near dropped the wood he was about to start a fire with. . . . It all turned out to be also a pleasant surprise for him, because as he came to tell me later, he was a town man, sure lonesome and seldom got to talking to anyone but brakemen for only a few minutes as the trains stopped for water. I was made very welcome, as welcome, I think as the good breakfast of bacon and eggs, hot biscuits and coffee was to me.

There was a train come by that morning which I could of taken but I was talked out of it. Besides I wasn't thru with my breakfast, and that coffee was sure hard to part with. There was another train come along about noon and I took that one. There was freights come and stopped but I never was no hand at hooking one of them or riding the rods.

I had to go quite a round-about way, by train, to get to the outfit where I wanted to go, where my horses was, about three times as far as if I could of cut straight across. I made two changes and it took me a day and a half to get there. But there was no choice. I got to the little cowtown which was my stopping place, and being the outfit had their business office in that town, I went there and didn't have to wait so long to get a buckboard ride to the headquarters ranch, where the next day I got a company horse and saddle and rode out after my own horses.

Most of the outfits was always very accommodating that way to the cowboys that had or would at times ride for 'em, the dependable ones, and they gained much more than they ever lost by giving such accommodations, for, the cowboy, whether he was riding for the outfit or not, always had an interest for its stock. Sometimes strayed bunches located so far from their range they'd never been found, was returned or word sent as to their location so they could be got. Such cowboys was as steady representatives without pay in whatever range or state they rode and there's where come the good accommodations from the outfit whenever such returned to its ranges.

I'd rode for that outfit at different times, and when I found my horses, on good range and in fine shape, and took two out of the six I had there and was ready to leave again, the superintendent, after my telling him how I come to been afoot, insisted I take one of the company's saddles, to ship it back when I got my other again. It was only a ranch saddle such as is used by the ranch hands to ride the irrigation ditches, irrigate the big hay meadows and ride along fixing fence. The one I picked was a pretty good one, sure a heap better than riding bareback the long distance to where I'd hung my own saddle up the tall pinon tree to the south.

I'd also left some tarpaulin-covered bedding and clothing stored at the headquarters' ranch. That all I hitched on my other horse, for I'd decided not to travel light for a spell. . . . With a pack horse and my bed I could take a bigger amount and variety of grub too, enough to last me for a month if necessary. So, south I hit again, all rigged up in good shape and free and independent as the breeze. . . . After quite a few days of good traveling across country, passing only scattered ranches and camps, and one freighter's station, or town, where there was a store and post office and at least six saloons, on the way I again got to the railroad tank and the lonesome town feller there. I stayed the night with him, when he about talked me to sleep, and before leaving the next morning I had him ship the company saddle back for me. I offered to repay him for the bacon and coffee which he'd so well fed me with but he wouldn't listen to that, only that he would like to have some of the jerky which I always took along. He'd never et any of that before.

From there on I rode bareback the ten or twelve miles to where I'd left my saddle up the tree. I made it further than that for I didn't want to take my horses thru that scope which I'd skipped and hopped thru, where the side-winders had been holding their sort of convention or reunion, while on my way afoot to the water tank.

So I rode around some thereabouts and must of got on the outskirts of the main gathering, for I seen only a few along by that way. That ride wasn't at all one I enjoyed, for riding even a mile or still shorter distance bareback was always that much too much for me. My very first time on a horse was with a saddle on him, never got used to ride without one, and if now my saddle come up missing from the tree where I'd left it I'd sure hightail it back to the railroad tank and get that company saddle again before it was shipped back. I would return it when I got another one of my own order and style.

But mine was still as I'd left it in the tree when I got there, and unharmed by any of the varmints that roam the desert. In a short time I had it on my horse and comfortably riding on again to the next water, which was the spring where I'd lost Monte more than a couple of weeks before. Thoughts of that horse came to me some more then. I sure hated losing that horse. He was young, big and strong and a fine cowhorse, also a very good traveler. I missed him, but I had no more hopes of ever finding him again, for I figured he'd wandered off to other ranges from that jackass and mule country, to where I couldn't guess.

It was late that evening when I rode up to the spring, and, to my surprise, I seen the light of a fire long before I got there, and then some men around it. I figured they was horse hunters making their rounds of the traps, branding the colts and keeping the ones they wanted for market from the bunches they caught.

I'd figured right, for that's what the men was there for. There was four of 'em, and I was greeted well as I rode up. They was plum set against my building a separate fire and cooking my own bait, inviting me to what they already had cooked. I was glad to accept the invitation and to partake of the meal that'd been kept warm in skillets and ovens set on coals scraped out of the fire.

I unpacked and unsaddled my horses first, took them up the mountainside to where the riders also had theirs hobbled, and felt pretty safe for the night that no long-eared jack would be setting me afoot as one had before. There'd at least be a few of the horses left to ride and we'd soon catch up on the ones that might get away.

Being them men done no riding in day time, only sometimes every few days to take whatever salable stock or others they might want to the main big corrals and pasture where all was gathered, or while moving to some other spring, they'd sit up, smoke and talk by the fire until later than most riders on other range work do. Their trapping of horses was mostly at night anyway, when they'd take shifts at the pit.

So as they sat up while I et my fill and feeling they was sort of curious as to my being in that country, where I came from, where I was headed and so on, I partly made up a story which, being it was without their asking, seemed to satisfy 'em.

But there was one part of the story which I didn't make up, and that was about and how I lost my horse Monte from this same spring. I told of his general description, color, age, weight and of the two brands, one on the shoulder and the other on the thigh. I asked if they'd seen or heard tell of such a horse. But none acted as tho they had, one of 'em remarking they'd just got to this spring that day themselves.

As I'd long before figured that horse to've rambled out of that country it was no disappointment to me to learn that they hadn't

139

seen him, and I again put him out of my mind as lost for good, as I crawled in between my tarp and bedding and went to sleep for the night.

I was awake and up at the break of day. The fire had been rebuilt and I went to join the two of the riders who was up and stirring a breakfast by it. . . . I'd just got to 'em when from below, by the trap which was out of sight, there come the sound of the heavy gate slamming shut.

"There goes another bunch," says one of the riders, "the second bunch for tonight."

At that sound and talk something made me want to go down and take a peek at the bunch that had just been trapped. As I come to sight of it my heart sort of missed a beat, for I seen what looked like a white horse in that bunch, showing much whiter from the new light of day and with that dark bunch. It would be too good to be true, I reasoned, as I come close to the trap and looked into it. But as I looked thru the twisted juniper posts there was no mistaking that roman nose, long slim neck and rounded body. It was all good and true, for there, as big as life, was my lost horse, sure enough, Monte himself.

I didn't lose no time in catching and leading him out of the corral, and looking him over I was as glad to see him as to notice how fat he was. He always kept in good shape if he had half a chance but this had been the fattest I'd seen him for a long time. He was sure good to look at, and that sort of made up for two now well-healing gashes on him, one on his jaw and the other on his neck, close to the jugular vein. The sure marks of a jackass's doings.

I think it was a good thing I was there just at the time that horse came in, for I most likely would of never seen him again. Them riders was great admirers of good-looking good horses, and Monte was sure all of that. It was another good thing too, I think, that I so fully had described the horse, brand and all, the night before, for I might of had trouble laying claim to him.

As it was, they was for trading me out of him. Good offers was made but there was no trading me out of him. They carried on with their trading talk most all the while I was eating breakfast with 'em, at their request, but as I laughed off all offers as useless they finally quit, and as a windup one of 'em had to remark, grinning: "Well, all right," he warned, "but you'd better not lose that horse in this part of the country again and I find him first. . . ."

That didn't happen. . . . The breakfast over with, I got my other two horses from up the mountainside, watered 'em good, saddled up and packed, and after a good-bye to the four riders, I got in my saddle, riding the well-rested Monte and leading the other two, headed on to cover the rest of the long distance for my visit South of the Border.

VIII

CLUBFOOT

S IT'S OFTEN BEING SAID that good men die young, it so goes sometimes with good horses. Such as them will get blemished and crippled for life while no account scrubs go thru hell and high water and bob up without a scratch.

Clubfoot was a mighty good horse, perfect build and size for a fine cowhorse, good head, and bright chestnut in color. He was breaking along well, getting wise to the ways of handling the ornery range critter, and was fast going up the ladder of what all is wanted in a good cowhorse.

Then it happened. Some hawnyawk (dry prairie farmer) had stretched a one-strand, barbed wire fence around a homestead he'd filed upon, right in the heart of good range land, and Clubfoot (he was named that afterwards) like all range horses and not knowing much about what a wicked strand of barbwire could do, got tangled up in that hawnyawk's fence, and being still plenty wild and spooky, fought against it.

With his active strength it was a wonder he got out of the wire entanglement without being ripped wide open. But there was quite a few cuts on him, and the worst, which crippled all the possibilities of that fine horse, was that he had a front foot near sawed off as he'd fought to break loose from the barbed wire.

The nighthawk (night wrangler) told me about him that afternoon as me and the other riders rode into camp after that day's second circle (round-up ride). He told me because that horse was in my string. I'd started him and had him to where he'd be all I figured a good horse would be.

The nighthawk didn't move the horse from where he'd seen him that morning. He'd thought it was best not to try, and it was. The horse had got free by then and how he'd got in the wire the nighthawk didn't know, for he'd been holding the remuda (saddle horse herd) quite a ways from that fence. Clubfoot must of grazed away to it during the night. And it's not always that the nighthawk knows of that in the darkness. There'd been no other horses with him when he was found.

Me and the nighthawk and a couple of other riders rode to where he was, and at the sight of him, his dark mane and bright chestnut hide speckled with blood and his standing in pain, on three legs, I wanted to wrap some of the barb wire around the hawnyawk's neck and string him up with it, but he wasn't in his pillbox of a frame shack. . . .

The chestnut wasn't easy to handle, but as careful as we could and using no more rope than we had to, we got him down as easy as we could. . . . So near sawed thru was his hoof that a cut of a knife, a little twist and it would of come off. . . . I doctored him.

There being seldom any medicines for horse or man in round-up camps, I made the cook sore by emptying what was left in a flour sack, took the sack, rode to where the main herd (cattle) was being held, just a short ways from where Clubfoot was, raked up some very fresh cow manure into the sack and rushed over to the hurt horse. The manure was still warm. I took his foot and eased it into that so the manure covered his whole foot and well up to above his ankle, the best medicine and treatment I ever found for such deep cuts.

I let him up to stand after that was done and he seemed relieved of pain some. But I didn't want him to move, and he didn't act like he wanted to either. He'd lost a lot of blood and, with all the strength he'd had, he was now weak.

Horse and cow outfits are usually very thoughtful of their saddle stock, much more so than with their riders. The sentiments was, and still are, that a horse is very necessary. So is the rider, of course. But if a horse gets his neck broke that's mighty serious to the outfit. If a cowboy gets his broke it's only too bad, another takes his place, and no wages lost. With a horse, the breeding, raising and breaking of him is a loss in cash.

Anyway, I took as good care of the chestnut as tho he was my own, brought fresh cow manure to his hoof at the crack of dawn the next day, and water, too. There was plenty of good grass around but he wouldn't put his nose down to it for that day.

That night, after another sixteen hours of riding, roping and branding, changes of horses, me and the nighthawk and another cowboy took it onto ourselves to dab our ropes on that barbed wire, and by the time we got thru we had that one strand of cutting wickedness wrapped well around that hawnyawk's shack so no more loose stock would get into it. We even coiled some of it inside, hoping he would get into it instead.

Maybe he realized some of what might happen to him if he showed up. Far as I know he never did. Just a sod buster gone back to where he belonged. Sure not in open range country.

The next day I ripped up some of the flaps of the cook's tent, getting myself in bad with him some more, and with another fresh batch of cow manure added on, the horse got to resting and even drinking out of a bucket, which range horses are not at all used to and very much leary of.

It was good that our round-up outfit didn't move camp for a couple of days. We had quite a herd, upwards of two thousand head, mixed stock and beeves. Our staying gave Clubfoot a chance, and I kept doctoring him steady before and after each day's riding, taking care of him in every way I could. For even if the horses was, and are, more precious to the outfit than their riders, I still felt bad that it had to be such a good horse getting so helplessly crippled while there was outlaws and jugheads going on without a scratch.

I done quite a bit of extra riding in caring for the horse, extra and over the sixteen and eighteen hours which was the regular day's ride, besides standing guard on night shift with the herd (cattle).

In the couple of days we made camp, Clubfoot, with the fresh "medicine" I kept doctoring him with, got so he could pack and shove that front foot ahead of him in fair shape, going the same direction he aimed it to. I had it well bandaged so he could.

Then the wagon (round-up) moved. Work had to keep on being done, and before riding away from that camp site I told the day horse wrangler to leave Clubfoot where he was, to not mind what the wagon boss might say, for the chestnut was in my string, and it's against any round-up boss to tell his riders as to what or anything to do with any horse in his string. Such doings is a plain invitation for a rider to quit, before he got fired, and a man that has to be told about the handling of his horses is soon fired anyway, if he doesn't take the hint and quit.

As the round-up outfit kept a-moving along as we rode each range I didn't get to take care of Clubfoot much any more. Before leaving that range I eased him slow to the creek where we'd camped so he could water as he wished, and good grass was there. He didn't have to move much to get his fill of both.

Then a couple of weeks later, as I was left to a line camp to ride from there every day, I went after poor Clubfoot and after a couple of days easy poking I got him to make the fifteen miles or so to the camp, where I went on to doctoring him some more of mornings and evenings. He'd got gaunted up and lost quite a bit of weight from the pain his hoof had given him but by the end of the couple of months I was at that camp I had him pretty well healed up and the hoof mended so he could at least sort of hobble to graze and water, and being there was no more pain he begin to fill up again some.

I quit the outfit that fall, rode on to other territories and for other outfits as I drifted. It was some few years afterwards when, without hardly realizing, I headed back and again went to riding for the outfit that owned Clubfoot, and, to my surprise, that horse was in the remuda and being used once in a while, in a pinch, and for slow riding, like with day wrangling or such.

He had a sure enough club foot but he could of stood quite a ride even with that handicap if it had been necessary, but there was no need for such at what little he was used for.

He was again fat as a seal, his bright chestnut hide a-shining as ever before, and being he was now rode so seldom, he'd developed

an ornery streak and, for a clubfooted horse, he could do a pretty
fair job of bucking, just plenty good for the kid wrangler to practice
up on to his ambitions of some day being a top bronc rider.

ONE DAY THERE COME A young stranger to the outfit. He looked about
eighteen, a couple of years older than the wrangler. We could right
away see he was no cowboy, but he wanted to be one and he sure
had all the loud and elaborate, wild trimmings. His peaked-hipped,
ewe-necked pony was of course a pinto, and that set him off well as
to how he figured a well-dressed cowboy should be rigged up.

He was a good-sized young feller, over six feet tall, and maybe in
time he would realize his dream of being a cowboy. But that outfit
had no time to break in any green hands, for they only bring on too
much extra work and trouble by doing things wrong and us having
to set 'em to rights again. So, and being a flunky was needed to help
the cook, such as with washing dishes, peeling potatoes, cutting
wood and the like, he was put to that.

The young feller was much disappointed but finally decided that
would have to do for the time. He could watch the goings on when
we was around camp and that way get onto the ropes. Then again,
he could sometimes get away when his work was done for a spell,
catch his paint horse and ride to where we'd rounded up and be
"working" a herd (branding and cutting out what stock was wanted
and throwed into the main herd which was kept herded to graze,
held day and night, sometimes a mixed herd to be shifted to other
range and then at other times beef herds that's gradually built up
with every day's round-up or drives, trailed to the shipping points
and loaded in the cars for market).

Boots we nicknamed the green hand on account of the size of his foot gear, so big that he couldn't pull his shotgun hair shaps (leggings, chaparejos) on and off over 'em. That evening he had to pull his boots off before he could his shaps, and each time pull his shaps on before he could his boots.

We got to having a lot of fun with Boots. His being so green left many openings for us which we couldn't resist taking advantage of. Many tricks was played on him while in camp or when he rode out to watch us at work with a herd. But most of all of them tricks was as a part of his education to his aim, some to play on his wit, and with the rough ones, none was so there would be any danger of any harm come to him.

There's never much for amusement on a hard riding cow or horse outfit, and sometimes what's called "laughing stock," some would-be smart aleck, is hired just for the purpose of keeping the boys amused by keeping him on the jump with catching jokes and tricks for him to squirm out of. It takes a long time for some of them to catch on, and when they finally graduate, they're no worse for wear and much better in wisdom.

We'd have some little fun with Boots that way, but he was so all good-natured that it sort of spoiled things for us, and when he'd sometimes get wise to a joke or trick we'd played on him, he'd take the play out of us by laughing about it as much or more than we had. Even the good standby as we had about his boots being so big that he had to pull them off so he could get his shaps off, or the other way around, got to be only amusing to him as a joke originator, and no matter what kind we'd invent, how good or how sharp, that only tickled his funny bone and left us helpless.

He was fast getting too wise for us to put any joke or trick over on him, and then there come something else to our rescue. That was in the shape of Clubfoot.

The wrangler having more chances and time than any of us to ride into camp, to just stick around for the company there or for a bite of sweetening, got to know Boots better than we got to, and when Boots could get away from his flunky work he'd sometimes saddle up his paint and ride to keep watch on the horses along with the wrangler.

Then one day the wrangler rode Clubfoot. He didn't need to, but Clubfoot hadn't been rode for quite a spell, and it was likely the wrangler wanted to show off to Boots some.

Clubfoot done his usual fair job of bucking and the wrangler was about a match for him, but no more, and that's when it come about that Boots remarked how he'd sure like to try to ride a horse that bucked, one that didn't buck too hard for the first try, and he wondered if he could ride Clubfoot.

The wrangler must of told him that there sure was no harm in trying, and maybe encouraged him some, that the foreman couldn't care because the horse couldn't be used for cow work anyway. So, on another day Boots done his first try on Clubfoot and the wrangler had to tell a few of us of the outcome of that try. Boots had stuck a couple of jumps, then, like a pivot was spun around up high in the saddle to be left to come down to earth all by himself.

We didn't see any chance for any digging jokes there, not for quite some time afterwards. . . . Boots didn't give up after being throwed the first, second, third and other times that followed, when Clubfoot tossed him off to sometimes nearly snap. He was all determined

Boots done his first try on Clubfoot.

and kept right on trying, and, whether Clubfoot got to slowing up some in his bucking or Boots sort of got the hang of his bucking and got to be a better rider, there come a time when he stuck on him one way and another about two out of every three sittings.

There was when Boots, figuring he could now ride good enough so there wouldn't be too many joking remarks come from us, started to doing his practicing to riding Clubfoot of evenings, when work was done and the remuda was corralled for the last time of the day, when we caught our nighthorses to picket 'em for use on our nightguard shift to holding the herd.

There was a couple of hours on till dark and time for the first nightguard shift of a couple of hours to each shift on thru the night, three to six riders to the shift, depending on the behaving and size of the herd, and weather.

Boots done his practicing on Clubfoot every third or fourth evening, and we of course gathered to watch the funny exhibition and pass our "comments" afterwards. . . . There was one thing Boots done every time he rode or was throwed that drawed pretty hard criticism from us, and that was that he always took and kept a death grip on the saddle horn from the time he climbed in the saddle till he was throwed or rode Clubfoot to a standstill.

No matter what we told him about grabbing and hanging onto the horn, what a disgraceful thing it was to do, how no good cowboy would ever stoop so low as doing that, and so on, he couldn't seem to help it and "went for leather" (grabbed the horn) every time Clubfoot unlimbered into action.

Then we thought of a plan to make Boots' riding exhibition still more funny. . . . We'd noticed that he had only a plain gray cotton saddle blanket and so we offered to bet him a colorful navajo, which one of the riders was the proud owner of, against his plain gray one that he couldn't stick Clubfoot five jumps, fan him with his hat every jump and not reach for leather.

Boots didn't have much to lose by accepting that bet and he'd sure liked to win the navajo saddle blanket, besides being able to do just such riding, without grabbing leather on Clubfoot and fanning him for five Jumps.

That bet stood for quite a while. It was too good a one to withdraw and not a rider wanted that cotton blanket of his. The bet was still standing when I again left the outfit a month or so later, with Boots steady trying to win it by riding Clubfoot every second or third day and trying his best every time to keep from grabbing that horn. But usually after the second jump, and, as we guessed, always before the fifth, during the time I was there, he'd reach down for the "old nubbin." That is, if he was still riding and to within reach of it. He'd usually quit fanning him after the first jump and drop his hat as tho it was red hot.

He couldn't somehow seem to break himself from doing that. We could see that he sure tried hard enough to, and we often had to laugh at the shapes, antics and positions Clubfoot would toss and twist him into.

There was a few times when it was mighty close "guessing" as to whether he grabbed the horn before, after or at the same time the fifth jump come. A bucking horse can make about five jumps in mighty quick time, in less than two seconds with a hard bucker, sometimes near impossible to keep track of or count.

We didn't try to be very accurate as to how many jumps Boots stuck before he dropped his hat and grabbed leather, we only rough-guessed, and the goings on being most always so comical to watch we'd sometimes forget to even guess. But we was usually safe in guessing that the fifth jump was about the limit for him to "stoop" to reach for the nubbin.

Boots' all seriousness and determination to make at least a fair ride against the high jolting odds and twists such as he'd never before experienced or dreamed that a horse could do, seemed to be his one big ambition. Riding Clubfoot for the first five jumps without touching the horn would mean one good start for him, and the winning of the navajo a sort of trophy as to that point.

With him being so determined to be the rider he wanted to be, we decided to help him towards his ambition that way by *making him ride* for that trophy. To let him have it too soon might of made him too satisfied with himself, to wanting a harder bucking horse and get really "busted" (hurt) before he'd get a fair start.

Besides, the cowboy who owned the navajo wasn't at all anxious to part with it anyway, and so, as the riding for it went on every once in awhile and Boots felt pretty sure a few times that he'd rode over the five jumps necessary to win, without grabbing leather, he was talked out of that and convinced that he hadn't fanned and had at least "touched" the horn, which amounts to the same as grabbing it for a hold. (That stands with the rodeo rules of today, and a contestant touching the horn is fined points, sometimes disqualified for doing just that, even tho it might be accidental.)

With losing his arguments that way being he never was so sure himself on account he was pretty well all over the horse every time he rode him and in about every position trick riders might get into, he kept right on trying, always determined to win.

Boots didn't realize it, but Clubfoot had got to bucking harder right along, while the boy only figured he wasn't learning or catching on how to ride a bucking horse.

With Clubfoot, to be saddled and rode, or *rode at*, only once in a while and only to have his buck-out was great fun, an interesting game where he felt winner and happy in bucking his man off. He'd never bucked any rider off before, not until Boots came along, and now he'd got as wild in his ambitions and figuring out ways of keeping on bucking him off as often as he could, as Boots had got serious and ambitious to make a good ride on him. It had got to be a sure enough contest between the two.

Come a time when, with new twists and jolts brought on, and Boots sticking more often right along, with the help of the horn, Clubfoot got sort of desperate with feeling he was gradually losing at the game. . . . He got so that when Boots stuck he'd sort of lose his head and go to blind stampeding, and even tho handicapped with a club foot, he could make good enough speed so he'd be hard to catch up to by any rider who might be a horseback and handy.

He got worse right along that way. And that finally was the cause of near being his death, also Boots'. It was a pure miracle it wasn't. . . . Camp had been made on a high plain, not far from an eighty-foot cutbank, a straight up and down jumping off place to a shallow creek below.

There was many such cutbanks along most creeks and rivers of that country, and riding that range so much, on all kinds of horses, we seldom noticed 'em, for much of any range country is mighty rough.

So, we naturally gave no thought to that cutbank as Boots climbed on for another ride on Clubfoot that evening. It was near a quarter of a mile away.

As luck, or fate would have it, Boots made a better ride than usual that evening, stuck like a leech, and Clubfoot, after seeing there was no bucking him off that time, got wild-eyed and broke into another of his blind-running spells, straight for the deep cutbank. Only the wrangler was on his horse and he had no chance of catching up and stopping the stampeding Clubfoot. It all happened so fast, and over the cliff or cutbank Clubfoot and Boots went.

A few of us got to our picketed night horses right quick and rode to the edge of the cutbank, thinking for sure that the eighty foot or so straight drop to the bottom would mean the crumpled end to both horse and man.

For fear of the edge of the dirt bank giving away, I had one of the boys hold me at rope's length to his saddle horn while I walked to the edge to have a look below. It looked more like half a mile than eighty feet to the bottom down there (we measured it some time afterwards and two forty-foot rope lengths hardly reached the bottom), and as I looked below I was surprised to see no crumpled heap of either man or horse at the foot of the bank. Then I was surprised some more to look across, beyond the creek and see Clubfoot, not only on his feet but loping right on and away. Now, of course, packing an empty saddle.

As for Boots, I couldn't see him nowheres. I got back on my horse and we all rode along the edge of the high bank for a ways to where the ridge rounded down to the shallow creek, then doubled back up along it. . . . We found Boots across the creek from the high cutbank, in a patch of reed willows and all stretched out, unconscious.

Over the cliff or cutbank Clubfoot and Boots went.

Surprising to all of us, he came to as we splashed water on his face. He was bruised up considerable, got a sprained shoulder and lost a lot of skin but it was as a miracle to us he was alive at all.

Also Clubfoot which a couple of us caught up to a short time afterwards. With him there was a limp, also from a shoulder hurt, which would put him out of the running for some time, and from his knees up to his chest, and nose to his ears, his hide looked like "grained" (scraped) rawhide and not a hair showed on them parts.

Debating on the outcome of the two as we rode out the next morning some of the boys got to figuring that there'd be no more buck nor stampeding in Clubfoot. That even if his shoulder got well again the last happening would have scared all the orneriness out of him.

It was figured too that it would work some way the same on Boots, that it would scare the bronc riding ambition out of him, feeling mighty lucky he'd got off as easy as he did.

I didn't pass no opinion as to the outcome on neither horse nor man, for, as a rule, and with hardened riders, such happenings are only taken along as all in the day's work. But in this case the horse was already crippled with a clubfoot, and the boy being so new and green might come to figure the game too tough, getting such a hard bump from the start.

It was a week or so afterwards when I caught up my private horses and left the outfit. The boy was still on the "hospital" list when I rode away, and Clubfoot, after being greased up good a few times was left out of the remuda to take it easy with a small bunch of range horses.

WITH MY USUAL DRIFTING, always hankering for the sight of new ranges, riding for this and that outfit, I happened to be riding into another new range, again looking for a change, when I struck a good size outfit, and who did I see riding in amongst the other riders that afternoon but Boots.

I didn't recognize him at first, for it had been three years or so since I'd last seen him, after him and Clubfoot had taken the high dive, and he'd changed so much since, lost his green bearing, showy rigging, and got to looking more as a hard riding cowboy should. I noticed too, that as I went to work for the same outfit he'd turned out to be quite a hand. The first hard bump on Clubfoot hadn't stopped him.

He'd went from flunky to wrangler, from one outfit to another, to finally graduate up to being handed a good fairly tough mixed string and put on as a regular hand. He wasn't as yet no top "ranahan" but he had the markings.

About Clubfoot, Boots said he'd recuperated and got in good shape again before he left that outfit, but he'd never been put back in the remuda, just left to roam with mixed range horses.

"I'll never forget that horse," he went on; "he started me, kind of rough, but he sure done a fine job and broke me in well."

IX

ONE GOOD TURN

CROPPY WAS A LITTLE GRAY HORSE I'd traded for while riding through a settlement on my way to another range country. I traded because I felt sorry for the horse, not because I needed him, for I already had a string of six good horses, all excepting one.

I was riding along and keeping my horses in a good walking pace when, glancing over my shoulder, I sees a horse and rider coming my way at the speed of a runaway engine. It didn't take the rider long to catch up with me, and I was surprised that instead of going on like I thought he would, on account of he'd seemed to be in such a hurry, he jerked his sweaty and panting horse, in a showing-off way, to a walk alongside of mine.

As we howdydoed I could tell by one glance at the rider that he was out to play cowboy. His outfit, from the rattlesnake hatband on his big hat to his leather cuffs and chaps, was all decorated up with nickel spots; there was more nickel spots on his saddle and bridle, and from all about him I figured that all his riding was done at showing-off in the settlement and none at all on the range.

"The way you're riding," I says, as we begin talking, "I thought sure you was headed to a fire, or maybe a funeral somewhere."

He grins and looks at me kind of blank:

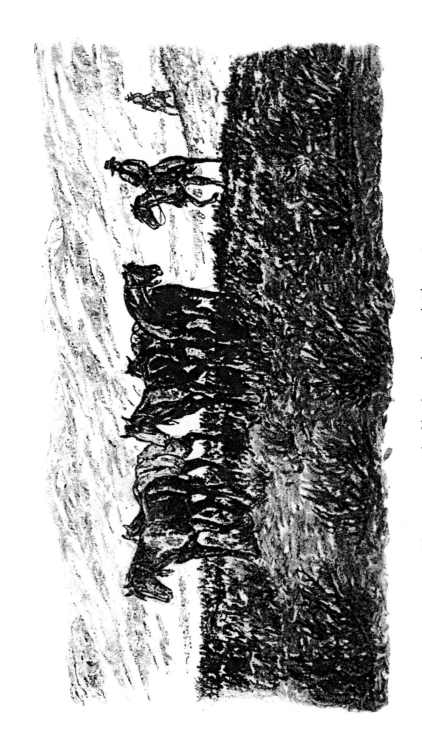

Glancing over my shoulder, I sees a horse and rider coming my way.

"No," he say, "I was just going after the mail." "Oh, I see, Pony Express rider." I went on: "But I still think you was headed for a funeral."

"Funeral?" he asks, surprised. "What makes you think so?"

"Well," I says, grinning sarcastic. "The way you ride that horse of yours there'll soon be a funeral, a horse funeral. Doggone shame, too, because he's a right pretty little horse."

"Yes," agrees the would-be cowboy, "he is a pretty little horse, and a good one, too, but I think he's too small for me."

We rode along, not talking much, and I noticed that that feller was sure sizing up my saddle horses, even the one I was riding. I had a hunch as to what that meant and I figured he would soon be talking trade to me, so I prepared for that and I sized his horse up mighty quick. I could tell he was a good horse and not too little for any man who knows how to sit a horse and treat him right. He was poor and tired looking, but he was young and sound, and with a rest on good feed he would be a mighty good little horse. I couldn't tell how well broke he was or how much he knowed, but I could see he was willing and not at all stiff-necked or stubborn. He seemed to be only anxious to do all he could to please his rider, and when I seen that his mouth was bleeding from the crazy looking bit he was packing, I decided to help that little horse and trade for him, if possible.

But I didn't want to let on that I would trade or the big hunk of nickel-plated meat that slopped on the little gray might of made the trading hard. I figured to let him be first to talk trade, and from the way he acted I didn't think I'd have long to wait.

And I didn't. He spoke right up, and, pointing to a big buckskin in my string, he asked how I'd trade him for his little gray. The buckskin was a good-looking horse but about as worthless as he was good to look at. He was too slow and lazy to catch cold, no spur could faze his thick hide and a feller sure had to work his way on him. He was stiff-necked and cold-jawed, and it was near as hard to turn him by pulling on a rein as it would of been by pulling on his tail. He was no young horse either, and outside of a ring bone that was started, and a sprained tendon, he was fairly sound. To a green-horn he would look sound enough.

I used the horse very little, only to pack once in a while, but never to ride, for I'd rode him once and that had been enough for me. So I kept him for a trading horse. I'd got him that way a couple of months before, and even though I'd got stung a little in that trade I figured I'd more than make that up in some other trade with him. The looks of him would sure do the work if I run acrost the right party to trade with, and now I thought I sure had that party.

I acted kind of surprised and not at all interested when the nickel-spotted feller pointed at my buckskin and asked how I'd trade for his gray.

"Why," I says, grinning, "you ain't riding nothing that would make trade, and you'd have to give me so much to boot with that skinny little gray of yours that you'd just about be buying that buck-skin of mine."

That seemed to set that feller to thinking and feeling kind of cheap as he looked down at his horse, for that poor little gray did look mighty puny as compared to my big buckskin. But I knowed that the little gray was easy worth two of the buckskin any time or place.

I didn't feel no remorse as I went on with my trading talk; in-stead I felt pleased with the hope that I could make him pay for the way he treated the little gray, and the more I could make him pay the better I'd like it.

"That buckskin of mine is some horse," I bragged on, "as good a looking horse as you'll find anywhere. He'd make you proud of being seen on him, and he'll go as far as you want to ride him any time."

That all was sure the truth, and 'specially the last part, because, with going any long distance, the rider would be more tired in making the horse go than the horse would in travelling the distance.

"He's a showy horse," I says, as I guessed the feller's caliber, "and would set off your fancy outfit nice. And another thing, if you want to show off in front of your girl and your friends once in awhile, all you have to do is "thumb" him (running both thumbs stiff along neck muscles) and he'll give a pretty fair exhibition of bucking, but not hard enough to buck off any average rider." That was only trade talk, for I didn't think the horse would ever buck.

"I know you sure can ride him, easy," I went on, not believing that he would ride any horse that bucked much. But that remark done its work and it sure pleased him.

The big buckskin, travelling ahead with my other horses, sure did look good. He carried his head up well and he showed good enough action. I noticed how the nickel-plated feller kept a-looking at him, and being as I had that feller's pedigree pegged down I sort of guessed what was running in his mind as he looked at the horse. I figured how he pictured himself parading on the showy buckskin in the little town of the settlement, making him buck in front of the pool hall or post office or wherever there would be people to watch him. Yep, he'd have a great time playing cowboy of evenings.

165

We rode on, neither of us saying anything for quite a spell, then, as we came closer to the little town, I guess he got sort of nervous at the thought I'd be riding on, and I could see he'd decided that he just had to have that buckskin of mine.

"How much would you want to boot with this horse of mine for that buckskin of yours?" he blurted out.

"Well," I says, acting surprised again, "I never thought of parting with that horse." I lied. "Wouldn't any of the others do?"

I wouldn't of parted with any of the others. But I knowed I was safe there, and he says: "No, the buckskin is the one I want."

"You sure know a good horse when you see one," I says, grinning to myself. "The buckskin is right classy and with just one look at him anybody can see he's a hundred-and-fifty-dollar horse, plum gentle, too."

"But I couldn't give you no hundred to boot," he says, showing his hand, "I only paid fifty dollars for this gray, but he's a good horse, too, and worth more."

"I don't think he's worth fifty now," I says, eyeing the gray, "but," I went on, like I was doing some tall figuring, "being I'm about broke and need some money to travel on I'll trade with you if you'll give me sixty dollars to boot."

If that feller'd had the money with him, I think he'd given me the sixty right then and there, but he didn't have it. He said he was getting only forty a month and board on the construction job where he was working, but he would do his best to borrow the money from some friends he had in town.

I said I would stay in town for the night and give him a chance to rake up the money. I was going to stay in town anyway, and he rode along with me to the feed lot of a livery stable.

There he left me, and, without even trying the buckskin, he hit for other parts of town to dig up the money. He'd gone by the good looks of the buckskin all together. That seemed to be about all that mattered to him.

I unpacked and unsaddled and left my horses loose to the hay manger, and, being it was near sundown, I hit for where I could get me a big steak. When I got back to the stable my trade victim was in the feed lot and looking the buckskin over some more. He looked kind of downhearted as he seen me and said that all he could rake up was thirty dollars.

"There's no splitting the difference in this trade," I says. "It's sixty to the boot or no trade."

I was running my bluff to the limit. I had a good chance and I took advantage of it, not only to please myself as a horse trader but to sort of even scores for the little gray.

He was bound to get my buckskin, and now he wanted to try him. From that I got the idea that he could rake up more money but he wanted to make double sure of the horse first.

The buckskin was gentle as a house cat, and as the feller put his saddle on him I remarked that I'd been riding the horse pretty hard and steady, that he was tired and maybe wouldn't show off so good right now.

"But to look at him," I says, "you wouldn't think he'd been rode much. He's a mighty tough horse."

The feller climbed in the saddle, and the buckskin showed lively enough as he was rode around the mangerful of hay in the big lot; he was even made to break into a trot and then a lope without much spurring, and I remarked once as the feller rode him past me that the horse sure looked good under that fancy outfit of his. That went well.

Another time that feller rode by me I told him to "goose" the horse and make him buck a little. I said he couldn't buck hard, and fact is I didn't think he'd buck at all. The feller looked at me kind of like he was leary to try, and when I just laughed, he got up enough gumption to run both his thumbs along the horse's neck. To my real surprise the horse did buck, not exactly buck but crowhopped in a few long lazy-like jumps and, of course, the feller rode him easy enough. That sure clinched the deal and the feller was as tickled as a baby with a new rattle. He seemed so pleased and surprised to be still on the horse after the last jump, that after he took a breath on that he thumbed him again and the buckskin crowhopped some more.

Then I thought that had gone far enough, for I figured that horse might loosen up, really buck and throw him off, and I wanted to get my boot money and make the trade before that happened. It was getting dark, too, and he still had to go back to the construction camp.

He got off the buckskin and, as I had made it plain that there would be no trade unless he raked up the sixty dollars, he rushed out saying that he'd somehow get thirty dollars more to add to the thirty he already got. I figured he'd sure try hard this time.

I told him I'd wait in the stable office. I waited for about an hour, and then here he come back on the run. He hadn't been able to rake up over twenty dollars more, and I knowed that he'd sure done his best. That made fifty dollars all together, and I accepted. I think I'd accepted even if I hadn't wanted to trade because he sure begged for me to let him have that buckskin.

We shook hands and he rode away happy on that horse, leaving me with the little gray and fifty dollars to boot.

If it had come to a showdown I'd of been glad to trade my buckskin even up for the gray, and given some boot myself, if I'd had to, and though I didn't need the gray, I liked him a heap better than the buckskin, and I wanted to save that good little horse from more abuse. I'd evened up scores for him, and as for the buckskin, that horse's hide and head was too thick to feel any abuse. He'd be sure to always take good care of himself.

It was early the next morning when I lined out, the little gray free with my other horses and with no other meat to pack but what little was on his own bones. I took some grain along in the pack for him, and when the settlement was left behind and I made camp in open country again, I gave him a good feed of that grain before I hobbled him out to graze. I hated to hobble him but he was still too close to where he'd been used to and I was afraid he might go back or wander away.

When I first got the little gray I decided to name him Croppy on account that both his ears was cropped; half of 'em had froze off during some blizzard and only stubs was left. The feller I'd got him from called him Prince, I think, or some such fancy name, but Croppy, as a name, fitted him well for me.

Croppy was the closest horse to my camp when I woke up and looked around the next morning, and I gave him another good feed of grain before starting out for the day's travel. He was still free to nip at the scattered bunch grass as he went along with my other horses and he had nothing to pack but his own self.

A few days' travel from the settlement and I come to the round-up camp of a big cow outfit. I went to work for that outfit, turned my horses in the "caviada" (saddle horse bunch) and they had nothing to do but eat and rest and pile on fat while I rode the outfit's horses on round-up. That was a good outfit and I stayed on for some months, longer than I usually stayed with any outfit, because the fever to drift on to new ranges would most always hit me after I was with an outfit for a couple of months.

I didn't neglect little Croppy as I rode on for the outfit. Him and my other horses was in the caviada which was corraled two or three times a day while we changed horses and I got to see him every time the caviada was corraled. Croppy didn't need no care but being he was a little poor at first and I run out of grain, I begin feeding him pieces of biscuits which the riders throwed away after they got through eating. The little son of a gun got to liking 'em real well, and come a time when there wasn't enough pieces of biscuits on the ground, I'd nip a few from the Dutch oven, and sometimes, when the caviada would be turned out of the corral, he'd hang around camp till I gave him a biscuit before he'd join the bunch to graze.

I never was much to make a pet of any horse. I always take the best of care of a horse and I leave him alone when I don't need him. Most pets are only doggone nuisances and spoiled, sniffing in pockets or chewing on saddle leather. None of my best horses ever cared to be petted.

Croppy could of been spoiled into a pet easy enough, but I wanted to keep him dependable, and the closest I wanted him to be to a pet was to have him so he would let me walk up to him any time or place, whether he was in a corral or out grazing with other horses. I couldn't do that with my other horses, and a horse that can be walked up to when he's out loose is mighty handy at times.

With Croppy liking biscuits the way he did, gave me a good chance to train him to let me walk up to him when loose and even when he might of wanted to run away to other horses. I'd ride through the caviada every chance I had and finally got him so I could walk up to him and he'd wait for me even if the other horses around loped away. Sometimes, coming in from a long ride, I didn't have no biscuits to give him and he'd let me catch him just the same, but I'd make up for that at other times. He'd got to be quite a camp horse, too, and often stuck around close, when the caviada was grazing a mile away.

There come many times when my training Croppy not to run away from me when loose turned out to be mighty handy, and the first time was when I quit the outfit and hit out for other ranges. Croppy, like my other horses, was now fat as a seal.

I was a couple of days' ride away from the outfit's range, and night was coming on when I made camp by a corral and up in some hills above a spring. The best feed was up there, but it was scarce most everywhere in that country, and I was careful to hobble all my horses so they wouldn't drift too far, all but Croppy, for he never tried to lead the horses away nor would he leave them. I gave him a cold flapjack which I'd cooked that morning and then he went to grazing.

When I crawled out of my bedding the next morning I couldn't see any of my horses anywhere, but I didn't think much of that because, as often happened, they would only be around the point of some hill and close by. So I took my time to cooking myself a breakfast and getting my stuff ready to pack before I went to looking for them.

I picked up their tracks and followed 'em to where they'd grazed over a low ridge. I thought sure of finding them on the other side, but they wasn't there, and they wasn't on the other side of the next ridge either, nor the next. I got up on top of another ridge and from there the tracks headed straight for a wide valley where there was no feed for a horse to stop and graze. I could of seen horses or their dust for ten miles and there was no sight of either. They'd sure hit out. I was afoot, and in a mighty big country. But there was nothing for me to do but keep on their trail all I could, and when I found one and then another broken rope hobble which had wore thin on the stiff brush, I sort of lost all hope of ever seeing my horses again, for I figured I'd find more broken hobbles along the trail and I'd never be able to catch up with 'em, not afoot.

I'd always prided myself of never being left afoot, but this was one time when it happened.

I started picking my way down off the rocky ridge, my thoughts far from cheerful, when, coming around the point of a rocky ledge what do I see, and only a rope's length from me, but my little Croppy horse.

How I felt at the sight of him can't be described with words, only that if a feller had come to me right then and wanted to trade me a hundred buckskins for that little gray, I'd been apt to take a shot at him.

That little horse had left the other horses go on and was coming back to my camp to get his biscuits but biscuits or no biscuits I don't think he'd ever come back to the feller I'd got him from.

It was only a couple of miles back to my camp. I rode him there bareback, and without even a string on his head. I'd left a couple of

How I felt at the sight of him can't be described.

flapjacks on a rock for him, and while he et them I saddled him and then started on the trail of my other horses. I was well mounted on little Croppy and by the time night come I had them runaways back to my camp. I made sure of new hobbles which I cut off a heavy cotton rope for 'em, and I "side-lined" two of the leaders to make double sure I'd have 'em when morning come.

Croppy didn't get no hobbles, only an extra mess of flapjacks. If I done that little horse a good turn when I got him away from the horse-killing hombre he sure more than repaid me, not only that once but more times after that and in other ways.

X

BOARHOUND (A CIRCLE HORSE)

BOARHOUND WAS BUILT TO SPLIT the wind, like a butcher knife, and facing him he looked near like one, long eared and as tho both front legs came out of the same hole. But from the side he wasn't a bad looking horse, high withered, deep chested, with short back for his height and good sloping hip.

He was sorrel in color, never poor and never fat, whether he was steady under saddle or knee deep in blue joint. Hardly any ride could be too long for him and he could do a fair job of bucking. But on account of his being so limber and active he sometimes didn't have to buck to make a feller ride.

He'd make me ride that way most every time I'd line him out on circle (round-up ride) and even tho he was hard to set at such times, I'd give him his head and let him be free to do as he pleased for I enjoyed and laughed at his actions as much as he seemed to enjoy putting 'em on.

It was at such times when us riders was "scattered" to comb the country for stock to be brought in to the round-up grounds. At them times and while I'd be riding alone, he'd be as quick and sometimes quicker to spot stock as I would.

Boarhound had a wild horse instinct in him that never died and there was no moving creature, from a bug to a critter or rider, from a few feet to miles that he somehow didn't always spot first and before he himself was spotted.

A snake couldn't raise a head but there come a sudden twist in him to make me pay attention to my riding, the wiggling of a jack rabbit's ears sticking over a sage brush brought on the same action, or anything else he sighted sudden that way, even the crack of a twig. He was no brush horse, the higher and more open the country the better he liked it.

At first sight of any stock at a distance he'd sort of petrify to a stiff standstill and he wouldn't move until, from that distance, he could make out what the critters, or whatever the object, was. A prospector's tent or camp had him making circles and hitting for high places so he could get a good look at it, first, and before going on. With his wildness, he was full of curiosity, like an antelope, and that had to be satisfied.

As I'd let him have his head at them times I'd have a lot of fun in watching his actions, reactions, and staying in the middle of him the while. He was as tho he was free, plum overlooked *the fact* that there was a saddle and rider on him, and went on in his own wild, watchful and inquisitive way.

With the free rein I gave him he wasn't for ambling along in no low or boxed in ravines or canyons when he spotted any moving object, but would hit for where he'd have a good view and open space around to get away in in case he'd want to.

About the best was when some rider would top a rise at the back of him. Then was when he'd put on his wild horse act for fair. He'd be all a-quiver the second he'd glance back and see the rider, his head and tail would come up as he'd whirl like on the tip of his toes to face him. His eyes a-shining and nostrils opened wide he'd size up the coming rider for a few seconds, and then was when I'd prepare

176

to ride, for he'd of a sudden light out in a stiff legged, spine twisting pace that at one step would set me up to feel like a bird and the next to land like a ton of brick.

He'd keep up that stiff legged pace for a ways then circle to come to a jerky stop and face the rider again, to let out a loud whistling snort at him, and then he'd of a sudden hit out again, this time at full speed, head and tail up and for all the world like a free wild horse. (The horse had been caught from a wild bunch in that country.)

I'd let him run to his heart's desire. That is, so long as he went the direction I wanted. But after he'd have his little fun that way and I had mine, I'd take him to hand and we'd both settle down to work.

The only work Boarhound was ever fitted for was on circle. He was more than ten years old when I went to riding for the outfit he belonged to and was turned over to me in the string I was handed. He'd been rode for six years or so by then, right after stock all that time, but he'd never took to handling 'em. He could be made to turn an animal but not in quick time, and a dodging one could easy enough break past him. But for what he lacked at that work he more than made up in good, long and fast circles. He sure did like to head off horse or critter that was trying to get away from him and the faster they ran the better he liked it.

In all the years he'd been rode he never really gentled, and that wasn't from abuse, for that's not tolerated on any good outfit. No real cowboy will ever do that anyway, and besides there's no time for such.

After some few months' rest and at the start of every round-up, Boarhound near had to be tied down before he could be saddled

He'd of a sudden light out in a stiff legged, spine twisting pace.

the first time or two. It was never safe for anybody to come near him very sudden, and as I remember one time, when a feller who I hadn't seen for some years started walking up to me while I was a-straddle that horse.

He came up to within arm's length of Boarhound's shoulder and as he stuck up his hand to shake mine, Boarhound took it onto himself to do that for me, with a striking front hoof, and before I could hold him and that feller could get out of reach, he struck him a glancing blow on the chest and tore all the buttons off his shirt, also some of the shirt.

That feller was a fair cowboy, too, but his being so surprised to see me, he'd rushed up and was caught unawares.

But that same feller, Jimmy, I forget his last name, got to know Boarhound some more after that, for he went to work for the outfit, and as we all had plenty of horses and the outfit was short of good hands at the time, we all agreed to each chip one horse from our string to make him one.

A rider's company string is practically the same as his own while he's riding for the outfit. He has all the say over every horse in it, and the foreman, superintendent or even owners, are not supposed to use any of the horses without the rider's consent. To do that, on a regular outfit, means an insult and invitation for that rider to quit before he'd get fired. Being plain fired was an honor as compared to that.

Anyhow, on being asked, the most of us agreed to lend one horse out of our string to set Jimmy up. None of us wanted to be hard on him, the only thing, and natural like, we didn't care to part with any horse we thought the most of, but we didn't give him the meanest because some of our meanest was the best, in their own line of work.

But as consequences is, a rider hiring out the way he did, to have his string made up from other riders' string, had to be quite a rider. Jimmy was a fair one.

From my string I handed him Boarhound, not on account that I didn't like the horse, but he was one in my string that didn't care who rode him. To that horse one rider was the same as another, he had no consideration for any and he'd always take care of himself.

I had some rougher ones I could of handed Jimmy, but they was coming along (breaking) good and they'd got to know me pretty well. It was a couple of days before Jimmy dabbed his line on Boarhound. He'd got along with the other horses fairly good up till then, and recognizing him as the horse that'd near tore his shirt off as he came to meet me the few days before, sort of put a crimp in him from the start with that horse.

Noticing that, and being a friend of Jimmy, I told him he had nothing to fear from that horse, that he'd already rode worse ones than him since he'd been with the outfit and that this horse's actions was much worse than he really was.

I was telling the truth too, but that didn't seem to brace Jimmy up any, for old Boarhound liked to done his best to make a liar out of me. He was a-plenty to make any rider hesitate some as he naturally was, but as this new one pulled his rope on him, he looked all like for exterminating him, much worse, it seemed, than he'd ever been with me.

But maybe it was the way he was handling him, and the horse knew he was scared, where with me, not having any sense, and paying no attention to him maybe was the reason why he didn't act up so much.

Anyway, that horse did make a scary picture as the new rider came along the rope to him. His neck was arched high, his eyes glaring and his nostrils rolling with snorts, a wicked looking head. As to his wiry body, it was tense, quivering and ready to strike, like a coiled snake.

Jimmy was game but he turned to me, and being the only one near right then, he says: "You know, Bill, I'm a married man now, with two kids, and I promised my wife to quit riding rough ones when we was married. I done that, and now I don't know if to tackle this sorrel or not."

That's true with most cowboys when they marry, but I near had to laugh at that as I stepped off my horse and said, "Why, he's just bluffing."

I helped him saddle and all went fairly well. But that horse, by his actions, more than by his true wickedness, had put fear in many a rider, and some fell off of him more from that fear of them actions than from not being able to ride him.

That rider did set Boarhound well while that horse had his usual buck-out and we all lined out for that morning's circle in the usual way, some riding hard and high and others riding quiet and easy. Me, I was doing just fair to middling.

The circle we took that morning was in rough and timbered mountain country, it had to be combed close and none of us was ever much over half a mile apart. I started out, pairing with Jimmy on Boarhound, and coming to some scattered bunches of cattle we had to split. I rode on up a gully while he rode up another to do the same, and I'd just got part ways up when I heard a crashing of pine limbs, and looking up the side of the hill I seen Boarhound bucking and a-tearing thru the timber and heading straight down my way. The saddle was empty.

I didn't have much trouble of riding alongside and catching the horse. Then leading him I followed his trail back the way he came, to where I rode up onto Jimmy all doubled over in pain and under a big pine tree. He seemed to've had the wind knocked out of him and after I straightened him out and he could talk again, he pointed above his head to a limb of the pine and went to telling how Boarhound had bucked under it and hung him up there.

I looked up at the limb and thought then that it was pretty high for even a bucking horse to hook a rider up onto, but I let it go at that and had about forgot about it when a week or so later and Jimmy was riding Boarhound again I seen where it didn't take no limb to knock him off that horse. Instead of that he went to reaching for 'em, and this time when Boarhound "broke in two" (went to bucking) again he embraced the whole tree as tho his life depended on it.

Fact was that Jimmy was scared stiff of that horse and he'd grab anything he could get a hold of to get off of him the second he went to bucking. That was queer too, I thought, because he rode and got along well enough with the other horses in his string that was much tougher than Boarhound ever thought of being.

But it's queer that way once a man quits riding the rough ones. Past scary experiences and hurts makes him more leary and cautious then than the man who's never rode or even seen a horse. When a man quits riding the bad ones he should stay entirely quit

182

or he's apt to get more hurt than any time while he was in the thick of it.

Seeing so plain how Jimmy was so scared of Boarhound I offered to trade him another horse out of my string for him. He was glad to make the trade, for a horse of his own choice, a meaner one than Boarhound was, and the queer part of it was that he had no fear of that one and got along well with him.

I was sort of glad to get Boarhound back, for I missed his antics, and even tho he didn't seem to have any special liking for any rider, I think he favored me some for the way I'd let him have his play at freedom while riding him. That accounted too, I think, for his seldom ever bucking with me while out on circle.

I stayed on with that outfit until the fall works and beef shipping was done, and one day, after the last stock car was loaded, us boys caught fresh horses and rode on into town to celebrate some.

We was riding our showiest and spookiest horses. I was riding Boarhound, and even tho he wasn't so much for showy he was plenty for spooky, especially in a town. That horse had seen mighty few buildings of any kind in his life, and like many of his kind he'd never been in a stable.

I stayed in town that night, for a general clean-up, hair cut, and then took on most all that goes to make a town hum. It was away after the middle of the night when I finally decided to turn Boarhound loose in the livery stable feed corral. I then headed back for town, for I wasn't thru there yet.

It was near noon the next day when I went down to the stable and saddled up Boarhound, and being I'd bought some shirts and other necessary stuff, I rode up town to gather the packages. I was coming out of a store where I'd got some tobacco when I near bumped into an old lady with her arms so full of packages that she could hardly see me, and I could hardly see her for them either. But I ducked in time, and as I held the door open for her and seen the load she had I couldn't help but offer to pack some of it for her.

As she had quite a ways to go she was glad to accept, and then I of a sudden realized that I'd put my foot in it, for Boarhound wasn't the kind of a horse you could pack things onto, you done well to pack yourself on him, without any extras. I wasn't very good at packing things afoot myself, but as I was in for it, and when the old lady told me how far she lived I figured to somehow make Boarhound do the packing, along with also packing me. I figured it wouldn't of done to lead him because then he'd sure scatter things. I'd need to be in the middle of him, keep his head up and to behaving, if possible.

I blindfolded him before I went to tying on some of the heaviest bundles, and by the weight of 'em I wondered how the old lady had ever expected to make it home with such a load. I relieved her of a gallon vinegar jug, a ten pound sack of flour, a side of bacon and a few other packages which all I tied to my saddle strings, front and back.

Then I eased into the saddle, and I was just about to pull the blind off Boarhound's eyes when the old lady held a paper bag out to me, asking me if I could pack it too. There was a dozen eggs in that bag.

I had a hunch that all wouldn't be all well when I raised the blind with that paper bag in my one free hand, not mentioning the other stuff tied to the saddle which I figured would alone be mighty apt to spook Boarhound aplenty.

But to my surprise he was afraid to make a false move as I lifted the blind and he glanced back at me and all that was tied onto the saddle. He started on, stepping light and careful, as tho something might explode anytime if he didn't watch out, and all would of maybe went well when, all of a sudden a kid busted out from the back of a buckboard on a bicycle, and then's when Boarhound done the exploding.

First, he near kicked that kid off his bicycle, then he went on to see of what all he could get rid of that was fastened to the saddle. The vinegar jug was pounding him on the neck and that done everything but quiet him. The other packages went to rattling and a-flopping, and me, with one hand up and holding a bag of eggs, I was afraid to reach down to pull up on the reins for fear of breaking them eggs.

Once Boarhound tore loose into bucking he was for getting rid of everything that was on him, including me, and even the saddle, if he could. I was quite some handicapped holding that bag of eggs up in the air while the other stuff was pounding from all sides, and I was doing some tall riding.

I kept on doing some tall riding, figuring he'd soon let up, but there was no let up in him right then. Instead he seemed to get all the more determined to shedding off everything that was on him and I got to riding higher and higher with every jump.

There was quite a few people stepped outside the store, hotel and saloons by that time to watch and enjoy the goings on, and feeling myself slipping and not wanting to get bucked off in the middle of the street and in front of that audience, I proceeded to make use to a good advantage of what was handicapping me. That was the bag of eggs.

I reversed my hold on that bag, and using it like for a quirt I brought it down along Boarhound's neck, on one side and then the other most every jump he made. With doing that I got back into my saddle again, and then the bag begin to leak.

The eggs was well scrambled in a short time, shell and all, and as the bag went to leaking and I kept a-pounding Boarhound along the neck with it, the eggs splattered well along his neck and mane, on down to his foretop, ears and eyes, until he could hardly see any more for them.

Then he let up, and as I got him to behaving again and I took tally on my pack, I seen that everything was still riding, even to the vinegar jug. Everything but the eggs was accounted for, and noticing the half scared old lady standing against a building, I rode back to the store and got her another bag of eggs.

His fun over with, Boarhound then behaved well enough and the second batch of eggs and other stuff was delivered at the old lady's place in good shape. But the first batch of eggs which I'd scrambled on him dried and caked along his mane to foretop and ears. That omelet stuck there quite a few days and he had to roll quite a few times before it finally wore off.

I come near changing his name to "Ham-and" on account of that happening but decided that after all Boarhound still fitted him best, for one thing he was built like a razor-back javaling boar and another he was just as wild and as wicked. But, with all of that, he was a mighty good circle horse.

The eggs splattered well along his neck and mane.

XI

HIPPY (A NIGHT HORSE)

IPPY WAS THIS NIGHT HORSE'S NAME. He'd been named that before he was broke, on account of getting jammed against the heavy gate log of a corral while going thru too fast and a hip was caved in. It was some months later when he was run in again, and even tho he looked some lop-sided with the caved-in hip, it didn't seem to hinder him in his action. There wasn't a limp nor even a catch in his gait, but figuring that he wouldn't do for a long ride he was broke for use as a night horse.

What we call a night horse is one we ride on "night guard," in holding a herd of cattle which is to be moved on to other ranges or shipped to market. With most of the big outfits the night horse is used on night guard only, for there's a herd to be held most every night, sometimes the year around. The herd is worked over (culled out) during the day as different ranges are reached, and replaced by others from every day's round-ups, so there's always a herd to keep guard on, day and night. It's called a main herd or Manada.

The riders take shifts to holding the herd. During the day, three or four riders take on an average of six-hour shifts loose-herding the herd to grazing while the other riders go on circle, rounding up more stock in the surrounding country. The dayherd shifts comes on an average of every two or three days for each rider, depends on the amount of riders the outfit has and the size of the herd and kind

Even tho he looked some lop-sided with the caved-in hip, it didn't seem to hinder him in his action.

of cattle that's being held. No cowboy likes day herding, for you're not supposed to go to sleep on the job and there's seldom enough to do to keep you from doing just that.

But on night guard, when the herd is close-herded, every rider takes his two-hour shift regular and every night, and it might sound sort of queer, but few seem to mind that as much as day-herd, nor the break of sleep to ride the two hours' guard shift around and around the herd. Maybe it's on account of the many thoughts and dreams that comes to the mind at such times, by the quiet bedded herd and under starlit skies. That would be a good setting for these modern cowboy songs, and there's many such nights. But there's also as many of the other kind, when the skies are cloudy and all is dark as stacks of black cats in dark caves, when hard driven sleet and snow keeps the herd drifting, or with blinding lightning and roaring thundering and hurricane-like winds, cloudburst-like rains with hail pelting the hides of the restless cattle, to sometimes cause 'em to stampede.

Some night horses, if of quiet enough nature when colts, are started on the work of night guard right away after the first few saddlings and kept for that work only. A horse that's good for that work is as important as a horse that's good for cow work, such as cutting out roping, etc., and horses that's broke to night guard that way are usually mighty good at it, sometimes beyond human understanding.

Hippy was such a horse, and like with other such horses I've rode, he'd often make me wonder at his supernatural-like instinct or sixth sense. Like for instance, while holding half wild herds during pitch dark nights when I could hardly see his ears and the herd would be quiet and still, some of the cattle getting mighty wise and tricky would watch a rider go by and then sneak out of the herd as quiet and careful as a cat could. Once out of hearing distance from the herd, they would then go faster and faster until they safely made their getaway, when they would slow down to a steady drifting gait. But not many would get away that way unless there wasn't enough riders for the size of the herd. For a good night horse sure wouldn't let 'em if he was to within hearing distance of 'em as they sneaked out. He'd take after 'em and sometimes long before the rider could hear or see them during cloudy and real dark nights. As I'd be riding Hippy during such nights, and relying on him so much I'd once in a while half doze in the saddle, he'd sometimes near slip out from under me as with a sudden jerk he'd light into a tight run.

He'd be running from the herd, and like he was sure enough out to head off and turn some hard quitters and I of course would let him go, even tho in the darkness I couldn't see a thing ahead. But soon enough I'd be hearing the clicking of the critters' hoofs, for by then, knowing they'd been discovered, they'd hit out at top speed and try to lose us in the dark.

But there'd be no losing of Hippy, and soon enough he'd be alongside of the leader, then the bunch would be turned back to the herd. Seldom more than a few cattle at a time would try to sneak out that quiet way. These would be mostly old renegades, wise to all tricks, which had got away many times before when all would be quiet and the whole herd still.

There was times when it was pitch dark that way and Hippy would of a sudden burst out after some unseen herd-quitters that, riding alongside of 'em and getting to what I thought would be the leader I'd be for turning 'em back, but there'd be some such times when Hippy wouldn't turn, for there'd be another runaway bunch further on, which I couldn't see but which somehow he'd detected or got the wind of. I'd let him go, and sure enough, in short time I'd hear the clatter of more running hoofs ahead.

Having good confidence in Hippy that way, I'd leave it to him when come dark and stormy nights and I couldn't see very far. Where the renegades would run to when getting away from the herd would be towards the roughest of the surrounding country. Some of it would be rough enough for mountain goats, but Hippy fell only a couple of times with me during the three months I rode him on night guard for that outfit.

But an average bucking horse was easier to ride than Hippy when he'd hit out full speed and across rough country during them nights, for, in the pitch darkness, I couldn't tell for no distance ahead whether there'd be a sudden drop of some feet or a rise the same, or a jump or turn. I'd have to be doing some tall riding to stay in the saddle, for Hippy would take most any kind of country at the same speed and as tho it was all level, when he thought he was after stock that was trying to get away.

His instinct and hearing was so trained that way that sometimes I got to thinking he heard deer or antelope, or even cayotes in the distance, for there was some few times when he'd give me a wild ride, like he was after some runaway stock and there wouldn't be any, and when he'd finally slow down to a stop, and listen and realize that fact, it seemed to me he felt sort of foolish as I'd turn him back towards the herd.

Sometimes I think imagination got the best of him too, and he'd be mighty restless. But then, so would the herd be restless and, as I got to noticing, it would be mostly during such times when there'd be a stampede, maybe only a short scare, then again, there was some good ones too. Some of the stampedes sometimes broke loose after me and Hippy had been relieved of our shift, but I remembered that by Hippy's restlessness during our guard. He'd felt it coming.

That was the queer twist I found in Hippy, or maybe it was his just being over alert. But sometimes, while we'd quietly and steady make our rounds of the herd at a walk, he'd come to a stop, look and listen from some direction, sniff the air and then he'd start out, from a trot into a high lope. I couldn't see or hear anything, but knowing that with his developed senses and instinct I was no match for him at night, I'd let him go.

A few times it might of been only the crack of a twig or dry brush at a distance, and even tho he'd most always wind up by running onto some herd-quitters, there was times he'd line out that way when there wasn't anything, without scent nor sound to attract him. It would be just plain imagination or maybe he just wanted to have a run.

He did have some good chances to run during the few months I rode him, and when he didn't need to use his imagination for a reason. That was during some fair to middling to good, long-winded stampedes. Hippy more than enjoyed 'em, and would get so excited that he'd sometimes lose his head and stampede too, go to running wild and paying no attention as to where he was going or what he was running into. There'd be no turning or stopping him at such times. Then I'd figure he was a little "weedy," had inbibed in some of the loco weed.

The best and scariest run he put on that way for me was during one of them long-winded stampedes. It was a dark and spooky night. The herd at that time was made up of over a thousand head of big beef steers, from four-year-olds on up to near the limit of any steer's age, for two-thirds of the herd was "Mexico buckskins" (Longhorns) and there was no telling the age of some of them, but one good long summer in the tall grass of the northern range and they got as fat as their frame could allow, also as wild.

We was trailing this mixed herd of native and Mexico beeves to the shipping point, grazing 'em along the way and taking 'em easy so they wouldn't lose any more weight than possible. On that account we all was mighty careful so they wouldn't even get a start to stampeding, for the hard running and then the gathering of 'em as they'd scatter afterwards would cause the loss of quite a few pounds per steer, and if the stampede was a long and fast one, that would amount to a considerable loss when it come to over a thousand big steers.

All of us was doing our very best to see that no such would happen along the trail, with this herd, and all went well, until we got the herd about to go when, as we bedded the herd for that night, we noticed faint streaks of lightning away to the west and we picked out as big and level opening we could find to hold the herd in. It wasn't a very big opening, for that country was pretty rough, but it would do if the cattle didn't get too restless or start to running.

The cook had set camp in a well sheltered spot, close to a steep hill and well above the creek bank, but not under or very near any trees, for, as he remarked, when we gathered for supper that evening, he didn't like these so-late-in-the-year thunder storms.

"They're usually freakish," he said, "the wind is apt to twist and turn you inside out, and if the lightning don't get you a cloudburst most likely will."

It turned out that the cook was about halfways right in his prophecy. I was to be on "graveyard" shift that night. That guard is for the hours from midnight to two. But it was long before time for my shift when in the middle of what seemed to be a sure enough cloudburst, I and all the other riders off guard had to get out from under our tarps, jump on our horses and ride hard for the herd, wherever we thought it might be, for it had stampeded.

Every man was in the saddle, all but the cook and the day-wrangler, and they would of been riding too, only they of course never keep up night horses.

About eight of us rode on and circled quite a ways before we located the herd and some of the riders that was with it, and then it was only by the rumbling sound of the running hoofs splashing on muddy sod and the cracking of dry limbs as it went thru the scrub timber that we did locate it. That was between thunder claps. The flashes of lightning didn't help much, for they being so close near blinded us and it was only all the darker afterwards. Not mentioning the heavy sheets of rain that felt like to pound us into the earth.

The herd had of course left the opening soon as they first stampeded. When they leave that way they just seem to pick up and are gone, the whole herd as in one, and what riders are on shift have no chance to turn or hold 'em, not, from such a start, for it usually happens too sudden.

By the time we got to the herd it was scattered pretty bad and a rider couldn't tell whether he was in the middle of it or on one side with only part of it, or even in the lead. For there was cattle everywhere, running all directions, and in that rough, scrub-timber country there was no use of trying to get the herd together again, get 'em to milling and to stop. Not while that freak storm was raging on.

We done our best to find and keep on the outside of the scattering herd so they wouldn't scatter any more than was possible, but in that pitch darkness, heavy rain and wind and blinding lightning, we sometimes hardly knew where we was at. Our horses would slide down off slippery gumbo pinnacles and sidehills and right down amongst where some running cattle had piled up at the bottom. There was also the danger of more to come and sliding down, and a cowboy being jammed in at the bottom of a ravine or gully amongst hefty longhorns was likely to be there permanent.

But the big husky steers wouldn't be in no such a jam for long at a time, and slipping and sliding and running into one another, or trees and boulders, they kept a-going, fast as they could at the end, which would be when they got over their fright or became exhausted and couldn't run no more.

It was while the stampede was at its best, fireworks going on all around, thunder roaring on and rain a-pelting to the weight of an ounce a drop, wind a-tearing and all combined that me and Hippy slid onto a good sized bunch which I figured had split from the main part of the herd, and then was sure hitting out of the country.

All of us riders was pretty well scattered by then, as scattered as the cattle was, and hardly any of us knew where the other was. That sure couldn't be helped in that weather and country at that time. But scattered as we was we still worked together and to the same aim, which was, without orders or instructions, to always try to hold the herd together. If that was impossible, such as during that night, to ride for the lead bunches and try to turn 'em towards where the main part of the herd might be thought to be or towards the bed ground, where the herd had started from and was to be held for the night.

Figuring that the herd was so badly scattered and there was no main part to it I took to the lead of the big bunch I'd run onto. Hippy was all for that and slipped and slid 'em to turn after turn, running into bunch after bunch of more cattle, and cowboys all riding their best to turn each their bunches into a main one so's they'd be easier to hold. Me and Hippy was sure doing our share and sort of halfways enjoying the goings on when another bunch, like dropping from the heavy skies, slid right into the middle of the bunch we was already having a rough time trying to handle.

Well, there was nothing to do but get to the lead of *that* bunch, and if there was any weakness in that knocked-in hip of Hippy's it sure didn't show on him as he raced on and caught up with the lead.

By a dimmer flash of lightning I seen the lead as we caught up to it and somehow managed to turn the bunch back. I was about to hold Hippy down for a breathing spell then, but that bunch was no more than turned when he went right on, like he'd sure heard of another bunch getting away. I let him go.

It being so dark and stormy, having made so many turns and twists, down pinnacles and acrost flooded ravines and washes, I couldn't judge for very far just where I might be riding, but I judged that I was somewhere between where we'd bedded the herd that evening and where camp was.

There was a tearing sound of canvas, the breaking of a ridge pole,
and at that instant I knew it was the cook tent.

I didn't have much time to think of where I was right then, for Hippy had stampeded, or was running away with his imagination that there was more cattle ahead, and I was about to try to stop and turn him back when I of a sudden felt like he was getting out from under me and slipping down into space. I just only tried to steady him from falling then and, as good luck would have it, we hit the bottom right side up, still a-going full speed ahead. Then a tall white blur in the thick of the dark of a sudden stuck up in front of us, and at the speed we was going there was no chance to stop or go around it, and so right smack into that white blur we dived.

If it had been a stone wall it would of been the same. But there was a tearing sound of canvas, the breaking of a ridge pole, and at that instant I knew it was the cook tent. A flash of lightning at that same time made me see for double sure that it was.

It was again a miracle that Hippy and me didn't pile up when we hit that tent, but Hippy had tried to clear it and he hit it above center, and at the speed we was going the tent went down from under us, only bringing Hippy to his knees beyond it and to slide on them and his nose for a ways.

But he soon got his footing again and away he went some more, and I didn't try to stop him, not right then, for the cook who slept inside of that tent was mighty cranky at his best, just as handy with his shooting iron, and I sure didn't want to linger and let it be known whether it was me on Hippy, some other rider, or a hurri-cane that leveled the tent that night.

Nobody knows to this day, but if any of the riders who was with the outfit at the time happens to read this they will remember, espe-cially the cook will.

XII

THE BUCKING HORSE

I NEVER HAD FULL CONFIDENCE IN a colt that didn't buck some at the first few saddlings. In fact I was always leary of such kind, even after they was well broke and had been rode for a year or more. For I felt and still feel that it's just as natural for a good wiry colt to buck at first saddlings as it is for him to breathe, and to try to keep him from that is mighty apt to cause him to bust wide open sometime and really make a cowboy ride, and maybe throw him.

In this I'm talking of the western, range-bred horses which seldom see a rider and are run in and corralled only once or twice a year. Maybe it's in the air or in the range country itself but there's no horses anywhere else in the world, no matter how wild and free they run, that has the fighting and bucking instinct at heart or can begin to compare with our western range horses in that respect. Such a trait, or kink, might not be anything to be bragging about but, to me, I think it's a spirit that sure fits, and ought to be admired.

It's respected too by some of the poorer riders, and some of them will do considerable handling of 'em with different contraptions and ropes while on the ground, keep 'em from bucking all they can and then get in the middle of 'em after they think that's all out of their system.

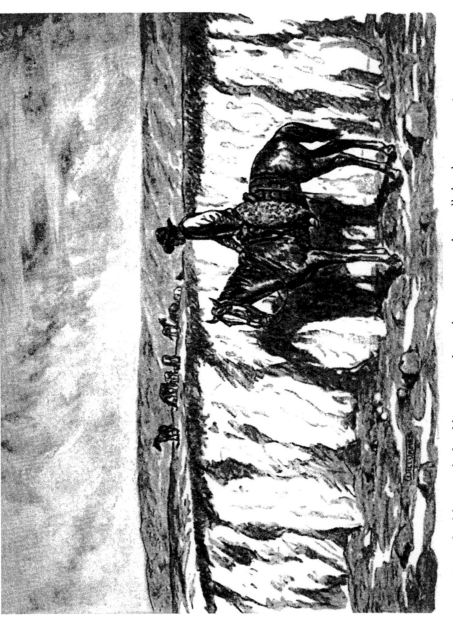

Range-bred horses which seldom see a rider and are run in and corralled only once or twice a year.

That works all right with some horses, and some outfits want their colts broken in that way, with the idea of having better behaving saddle stock, and so, getting better work out of 'em.

But I've never noticed much if any improvement with such outfits' horses that wanted their horses broken without a buck when possible. In fact, I've noticed that many such well-behaving broken horses would gradually get trickier and ornerier as they'd get wiser and older. Some would even turn outlaw and go to bucking for good, and hard, and I figured that on account of being curbed from their natural wants of ways of acting, that had stuck in their craw till it sort of soured, fermented and had to come out. And when they would bust loose they was much worse than they would have been if left free to have it out of their system during first saddlings, for then, being green, few could buck very hard and would soon enough see no use to that, that it wasn't getting 'em anything, and when that streak got out of their system they most all went to work all the better. Where with the older and well broken horse, when he starts in his orneriness, it's like with rebellion. He's wise to man's ways and he gets a lot of satisfaction from being bad, loosening or "unloading" his rider when good chances come and his "breaking in two" (bucking fit) is least expected.

A few of the old bronc-busters might not agree with me but I always like to see a colt have his buck out at first saddlings if he's inclined to. Most colts are, and they seem to feel better after that, like something off their chest, and more ready to take in other interests.

The few that are not inclined to I think should be encouraged some, not spurred nor made to, but given a free rein on a loose hackamore and spooked out of their tracks sudden, for even tho them few might not seem inclined, the buck is most likely there and sleeping for a later bust-out, which is usually a tough one. The spooking, sudden start, with the horse's head free, most always does the work of bringing the buck to the top if there's any laying sleeping in the colt.

I've always had good luck that way, giving the colts their head at first, and wouldn't start checking 'em up on that until they begin getting the idea that that was expected of 'em or that they sort of enjoyed it. Then, if they wanted to keep it up, I'd "whip" it out of 'em, not before or after, but while they was hard at it. The whipping wasn't done with a stinging or cutting quirt but with a two-inch wide doubled stub latigo strap eighteen inches long. A stinging quirt or whip would only be abuse and hurt, the colt to be apt to be mean or sulk, for with his bucking he's only going by his natural instinct and doesn't know he's doing anything he shouldn't.

With the flat latigo quirt popping loud with every crack of it on his rump, that only scares him out of his bucking each time he goes to it, leaving no welts, and comes a time when he gradually understands that bucking is not what's wanted of him. Then after a few more saddlings he usually forgets it. It's out of his system.

A few will keep up with their bucking after it's made plain to 'em and they well know they shouldn't. In such cases a regular quirt is brought on, one that stings as it pops, and then the ornery one gets a sure enough whipping, all according as to how mean he means to be.

Some will never entirely stop bucking and will light into it most every time they're rode for as long as they live. Others have natural mean streaks that's sort of bred into 'em, will fight every time they're caught and saddled, and buck until they're wore out, maybe half a dozen times before they're rode a mile from camp, and then no work can be got out of them. They're too all-in with fighting and bucking and have no interest in work anyway, nothing but fighting and bucking, born outlaws and of the kind that's used in rodeos for the bronc riders to take a sitting on at bucking contests.

It's figured by many people that the rodeo buckers are trained to be such. . . . Well, a horse that has to be trained to buck is never a good one, and it would sure be foolish and wicked to train a good behaving horse to buck when there's so many naturals that way that knows all the tricks and twists, learn more every time they're rode and whose interest is nothing but that, being outlaws, aching to buck, and to teach them how to do that would be the same as to try to teach an eagle how to fly.

There's always plenty of them to be found on our western ranges, from Canada to Mexico, and regardless of a few dams and farmed strips, there'll always be a powerful lot of big open country where such will be running.

There's usually whole strings or bunches of such outlaws with every big outfit. Horses that no work can be got out of on the range. The rodeo arena is their calling and there they're kept in the best of shape, strong and so the full extent of their bucking action and orneriness comes to the top.

The very false idea is that the bucking horse at rodeos is abused and gored into being what he is and mean. . . . The truth is that the bucking horse is very much better treated and cared for than the favorite race or polo horse or other stabled horses that are curried and brushed to the quick, fed and doped to run a faster stride before they're mature, just babies.

With the polo horse, he's more cared for as a horse should be, has more chance and is treated much like the cowhorse is. It's rough work, as is with the cowhorse, but more to a horse's natural lead than is with the race horse. There's quite a strain on the polo horse too, a steady training which the cowhorse doesn't get. With some race horses they're put to a training that practically kills 'em before they're a horse (full grown).

Where the good bucking horse is concerned, if he's a good one he's not brought into the arena until he's full five years old or older, not until that mean streak is found in him. That streak is not brought on by any gouging or mistreatment. For like with some humans, if it's in him nothing can be done about it and he's used to his best advantage that way. He doesn't get or need any gruelling training.

The prize fighter gets too much of that sometimes too—is usually a has-been at the early age of thirty by strenuous heart and hard work. Some are done for sooner than that. But with the bucking horse, his only training is to be on his native western range where over six months out of a year he has nothing to do but graze, wax fat, hold his wiry strength and hatch out more ways of bucking his rider off.

He's not taken off green grass too soon when spring comes, for that's a conditioner to him and he's not so strong for the time. But when the grass matures and is full of hardening nourishment, he sheds off slick and the tough sparkle is in his eye when he's loaded in the box car. Then grain and good hay fed to him, and he's very ready, with every muscle twitching, and aching to bust a cowboy. The gleam in his eye is far from abuse, only all challenging.

One of the best bucking horses I knew, after five years of pen-sioning, died at the age of thirty-two. That amounts to about the same as ninety years of age with a human, and usually twenty years is a good ripe age for any horse to reach. So that goes to show of the good care a bucking horse gets. It was claimed this horse never had been rode, but he was a few times. Anyhow, to his memory, that horse never felt he was ever rode.

There's a good monument built to that horse, one which he sure deserves as a emblem to our good American bucking horse, not hurt, not strained or trained.

Good, tough bronc riders stood while that horse was lowered under eight feet of sod and then granite boulders piled over him so he'd never be dug up. There was tears in some of the scarred and homely faces of the riders as that horse was let down with ropes, to rest, seal fat, with all the laurels of his conquests.

I've seen quite a few such good bad horses buried, with alms of Spanish bayonet—ones that had faithfully kept true to their high-twisting aim, fed up to it and cared for by the owners and good nature.

Every cowboy that knew, rode or rode-at them horses took their hats off as one such would be lowered to rest for more bucking across the Great Horse Divide, where they'd be again meeting their contestant riders.

THE BUCKING HORSE IS NOT a strain of any particular horse. The common idea is that the wild horse (mustangs) is hard to set and unbreakable, as the story goes about the zebra. But the wild horse is easier to break than the cross with a hot-blood (thoroughbred) and the wild horse himself.

The makings of our saddle stock, starting about eighty years ago, was of coach, hambletonian, hackney and a few other standards, little running stock, mostly trotters, long winded, with good weight to pack a rider and bust a heavy steer. They was good northern horses, from Oregon, crossed with the wild ones. Some of our best cowhorses was from the south, Steeldust and Comets, the first strain of our American horse brought over from Spain, and the breed kept alive and carefully strained from that stock by the first cattlemen of Texas.

As bucking horses go, I well remember one. He was one of them that was broke careful and with the buck held in him, and started gentle enough. He was from a throw of a hambletonian stallion whose colts all carried a mean streak.

With such crosses, range bred, is where our natural bucking stock comes from. One such a stallion, of any breed, can throw string after string of outlaws, few to ever tame so any range work can be done with 'em, even tho the stud himself might be mild tempered. A bad horse doesn't always come from a bad sire.

Getting back to this horse whose buck had been held down and near choked him, he finally busted loose, after two years of good behaving and getting to near be a top cow horse.

He was put in my string, with the colts I had going, and with the first sitting I had on that horse I seen that he'd turned out with a high aim, to fighting and bucking. His tension had sure enough broke loose.

After fighting until he wore himself out at every saddling, and no work could be got out of him, I told the wagon boss (cow foreman) there was no use wasting mine or any body else's time on him. That horse would rather died fighting than working, a born outlaw.

The main trouble, I figured, was that he didn't have his buck-out with his first saddlings, and, of course, the blood of his sire had a lot to do with it, too.

He'd been rode and behaved well for near two years before he "broke in two" and bucked his first man off, an old cowboy who'd quit riding rough ones years before, and that to him acted like the first taste of blood, or victory. Something he'd never tasted before, and got a thrill out of. So much so that as rider after rider tried him, he pined only for that and, as good a cowhorse as he'd once been, he'd pass up a cow critter as tho he'd never seen one before.

When he was turned over to me and I told the boss it was no use, he agreed and that horse was let go, to roam the range and pile up on more meanness.

Then a rodeo come to town. The horse was bucked in the try-out and he lit into that with so much hard pounding action that he was put in as a final horse, when the hardest buckers are used. The horse being so good was then sold to the owner of the rodeo stock for as much as a good cowhorse would bring, and went to touring the country, taking in the different rodeos the stock had been con-tracted for.

He done well in the arena, so well that he topped the string of buckers as the toughest and hardest to set. That horse was now right in the height of his glory and soon won a fame that made him the talk of the rodeo world. One horse that couldn't be rode.

He kept right up true to form and dependable with his bucking. There was none of the man killer in him, such as there is in many outlaws, but when a bronc rider came out of the chute on him there never was no doubt but that he'd sure have to ride and then some, in order to qualify or even stay on that horse. None did.

None did for quite some years. He stayed a top bucker, covering thousands of miles during the six-month rodeo season every year, taking in from ten to fifteen rodeos during that time and being rode or *rode at* from about three to six times at each rodeo.

After his many years in the arena, still bucking good as always, he was one day near surprised out of his hide, for there finally come a cowboy who stuck, and not only that but made a fair ride on him. That horse with the long years' record and fame of no one having ever been able to ride him. . . . And now he'd of a sudden met his waterloo, in one short contest between him and that wizard of a rider. That left the horse sort of dazed and like unbelieving.

The rider, of course, easy won first money for that great ride at that rodeo. And like a leach on the horse's trail he followed him on to another rodeo where, as luck or fate would have it, he drew that horse again for the finals, rode him thru to a good qualifying ride as the time before, and again took first money.

Well, that was the beginning of a fast end for the once unridden top bucking horse. For after being ridden the second time, when with desperate effort he'd brought out his wickedest jumps to no use, something snapped at his heart strings. For some days that followed he wouldn't eat and would hardly drink. He ganted up some but was rolling fat. A vet came a few times but there was nothing he could do. We knew what had gone wrong. Some of us had seen such symptoms with some wild horses after they'd been caught.

The famed bucker, all spirit and interest gone, standing in a moping, dejected way, stayed on his feet like in a trance that way for a few days and then one morning we found him down and stone dead. . . . He'd died of a broken heart. A true bucking horse at heart, the kind that's born and not made. He couldn't suffer being ridden, and if anyone could have been ignorant enough of horseflesh to think it was abuse that brought on his end, the sight of the good condition he was in at his death and the impressive ceremony of his burial would sure cleared all such thoughts. There was more genuine grief and feeling at that burial of the bucking outlaw, for the worthy opponent he'd been, than there might be at some human's burial. He was a proud bucking horse that had been much admired and later missed as much.

XIII

JOKER
(A HORSE THAT LIVED UP TO HIS NAME)

JOKER HAD ALREADY BEEN NAMED such before he was turned over to me, and a joker he sure turned out to be. For a horse he could get himself into more predicaments that would wind up into jokes on himself, including his rider, than most humans ever do.

He was a young horse, had been rode only a few times when I slipped my rope on him and went to work for the desert cow outfit he belonged to. I'd hired out to ride for that outfit and, as the joker horse he was, he fooled me the first time I laid eyes on him.

The foreman was in the corral with me, pointing out the string of broncs another rider had started breaking and I was to finish. Joker was one of 'em, a mighty well set up and good size blood bay, and running and snorting around the way he was, drawed my attention to him more than did the others.

Being a stranger in that country and wanting to make a sort of acquainting conversation with the foreman I asked him how much that Joker horse would weigh. He answered. "Make a guess."

It might be hard for some to believe but in some of the range countries, sometimes only a hundred miles or so separating, a horse of the same size and appearance will vary from one to two hundred pounds in weight, sometimes more. That's due to the kind of feed different ranges produce, also climate. Many an experienced horse dealer is fooled by the weight of a horse on that account, also by their age, for a horse from sandy, dry and brushy ranges will show a younger mouth than the one from the tall grass ranges and where running water is a-plenty.

As I've already said, Joker was a well set up and good sized horse and I made my guess according to the many such size and built horses I'd handled on other ranges. After I'd caught and walked up to him I guessed him to weigh eleven hundred.

The foreman grinned some. "I weighed him at the stockyards just a few days ago," he says, "and with saddle and all he weighed nine hundred and twenty."

Well, that was one at my expense from Joker.

It was on the next day when one of Joker's jokes turned on him. I'd made all ready the day before to hit out with a string of eight broncs, with only one gentle horse for pack and snubbing. The foreman had left me alone at the desert cow camp, figuring on making another such camp acrost a stretch of thirty miles and no water between (no distance for an automobile but no such country where an automobile could move).

To be sure of making that distance, along with driving my string of broncs, I picked on one in the string which I figured would have the age, and be hard and tough enough to stand up under the long and dry ride.

After the job of saddling and topping this horse, making it as I could so's to save him and myself, I opened the corral gate to start out with my string, the only gate from there to the camp I was headed for.

My string came out of the corral quiet enough, and then, a short distance down a dry wash, and all going well, this Joker horse of a sudden broke loose and like a bullet hit straight out for the horse range, where I'd got him from with the others just the day before.

There was no chance of heading him off. I tried but the horse I was riding "bogged" his head (went to bucking) and then stampeded another direction, no stopping him.

After finally circling him towards where my string had been, they'd also started, and going another direction from where I wanted 'em to go. With my horse now some winded, I maneuvered him so's to turn 'em. As good luck would have it, they'd stayed together, Joker being the only one missing and now very much out of sight. I had to let him go, figuring I would get him a month or so later, when I'd get back to the main camp again.

But such wasn't to be, not according to Joker, and along about the heat of noon that same day there come a streak of dust, and a blood bay horse making it. It was Joker. He'd made a circle of the horse range, looking for a bunch he was used to running with, and not finding it, had returned to the string, for there was two in the string that had belonged to the same bunch.

Joker had made quite a circle and covered more than a few miles by then, and he was good to stay with the string, behaving well until camp was reached. His wild break away had turned out to be a wild goose chase and a sort of a joke. To his expense this time.

ANOTHER JOKE AT HIS EXPENSE was when the foreman of this same outfit rode up to my camp and said that the owner (a mining man who knew a lot about ore and holes in the ground but nothing about cattle) ordered him to have me move to another spring camp

The horse I was riding "bogged" his head.

and run in what he thought was a weak cow he'd drove by and seen standing in the middle of a big dry and high mesa flat, with a calf by her side, dying of thirst, he thought, and starving.

I was having my hands full with quite a few hundred head of mighty scattered cattle at the time, and the mention of having me move to another camp to take care of just one lone cow and calf, more than made me and the foreman wonder and laugh some.

But orders was orders, and I sure didn't mind such an order because I'd been riding mighty hard for some time. Another rider took my place and my string, all but Joker. I figured he'd be just the horse I'd need for that lone and easy job, for, with his funny and tricky ways he'd sort of keep me company.

The time being winter and no stock running in that higher country, the owner had some grub and baled hay freighted some fifty miles in to the camp for just me, Joker and cow and calf. That and my time alone cost more than the cow was worth but that wasn't considered, nor any of my business, and right then I figured I'd have some easy riding for some days, at least until the owner of the outfit found out that all the cow needed was a good shove down country where she belonged.

The first day of my expected easy riding didn't start so good.— I found the cow. She wasn't exactly in prime shape for beef. If she had been she'd been easier to handle, and as she was, she was just in good shape to fight, and her husky calf was right aching for a good run.

The cow was pretty wild, and being alone with her calf that way, and the sight of a rider coming up on her, done everything but make her any tamer. I seen right away I'd have trouble getting that old heifer to the corral where I was to feed her, and I took her as easy as possible, staying a good distance away and not turning her any more often than I could help, for, by her actions she just wanted an excuse to get on the fight, and one turn or two too many would be sure to set her off.

I let her amble on pretty well as she pleased for a ways, and being I'd started her right, she headed on near the direction of the corral, only kind of at an angle. I let her amble on that direction for a ways, figuring on turning her when reaching the head of a dry wash which started from the mesa, wound thru the jack pine and led on down to near where the corral was.

Spooky cattle often take to down country well, especially a wash, and if the rider sort of keeps out of sight they'll sure ramble on in trying to lose him and not try to "brush" on him.

Joker was working good, and when the right time come I spurted him onto her so sudden that she just like sort of fell off the rim and into the head of the wash without looking where she was going or hesitating to want to fight, and down country she went, hers and her calf's tails a-popping.

All was going fine and I kept my distance. But the fun wasn't over yet. It hadn't even started, for getting the both in the dilapidated corral that was down some miles and at the edge of the wash, would still be the hardest to do. The short wings of the corral was about as good as none, and to make it still more ticklish there was some inches to a foot coating of ice at the only gate, all over the corral and on down past it a ways. That ice had formed from a spring above it, and that camp and corral seldom being used, the run of the water from it took its own course.

There was a small shed at one side of the corral where the supposed-to-be poor cow and calf was to be put and it was up to me to put 'em there.

Being I hadn't crowded the cow none while she and her calf hightailed down the wash, only to get a glimpse of 'em once in a while and see that they was going right, they was sort of calmed down some when she reached the place to where I was to turn 'em towards the corral. The cow turned easy enough and went on peaceful, until she came to the corral and the ice, and then, as I'd expected, her calf of a sudden broke away and the cow also whirled to make a dash for a break. Expecting that, I of course had my loop ready. I had her too close now to let her get away. I piled it onto her as she tried to run past, at the same time put Joker to speed on thru the corral gate, forgetting about the coating of ice and his getting any footing there. But with the speed we went there was no stopping, and being there was quite a slope inside the corral there was nothing for the cow to do but swap ends and follow. The shed was at the lower end of the corral. The cow, now on the fight, even tho she was sliding down on her side piled up in the shed, right with me and Joker, all on our sides.

There was a crash, bang against the log wall of the shed as the three of us hit it all in one heap. With watching the cow's horns and the slack of my rope so I wouldn't get tangled up in it, I was pretty busy, and so was Joker, for he didn't neither want to be in such close quarters with that mad cow and her horns. When we all crashed into the log wall, there was enough impact so that it broke some and Joker went on halfways thru. He done the rest in getting all the way thru.

He'd got his footing from the falling logs, bark and all there was under the shed, and left me there with the cow. I didn't want her to go thru the same hole we made, so, I dodged her horns and tied her down before she could get up, with the same rope I'd caught her with and forgot it was still hard and fast to the saddle horn.

Joker no more than got out of the shed when on slick ice he again lost his footing and slid on his side plum to the end of the rope, drawing it tight, and now he couldn't get his feet under him so as to get up. So there he was on the outside and down, and the cow inside also down.

I had a hard time standing up myself as I went along the rope to him, and the rope being so tight I seen where the only way he could get up was to uncinch the saddle and let him slide away from it to where he could get his footing.

He looked kind of foolish after that was done and finally got to his feet again. But the only joke there was on him that time was how he sure wasn't going to bed down with that mad cow crowding him so close, and then afterwards hitting the end of the rope and get "busted" (thrown) so he couldn't get up.

Both cow and horse now taken care of, I made an opening in a bare part of the corral and didn't have too much trouble getting the calf in. But I was sure to change the course of that spring water right afterwards. The ice soon got soft then and in a couple of days the most of it had melted away, leaving the corral more fit to use again.

It was in that same corral some days later when Joker, acting funny, took another bust. For having nothing to do as it was, with all the good hay he could eat, he got to feeling more rollicky than ever, if that was possible, for he always was full of the old nick and plenty of snorts.

This time I was going to catch him, figuring to ride to another spring, more to pass the time away than thinking there'd be any stock there that would need attention. I tried to stop him so I could walk up to him but there was no chance there. I made a few tries, and seeing there was nothing doing that way I went and got my rope.

Feeling as good as he did, the sight of my rope with ready loop, acted sort of like a fuse to the dynamite that was in him, and before I could get to within throwing distance of him he just sort of bounced, like a spooked antelope, and hit for the dilapidated but tall corral gate—He hit it plum center and high, but not clearing it, and with the force and speed he hit it the gate crashed to splinters. At the same time, his knees caught on the top pole which up-ended him to land out quite a ways and to a mighty hard fall.

It all happened so quick that all I done was stand in the corral with sudden thought that there I was without a horse, afoot, for, knowing his tricks as I did, I figured he'd jump right up and hightail it down country. There was only one fence in that part of the desert country and that was the corral fence, then it was all open (and still is) till the next corral miles away was reached, no pastures.

But to my surprise, when Joker jumped up, looked around kind of dazed and then spotted me inside the corral, he bowed his neck and jumped right back over the gate he'd splintered just a few seconds before, and into the corral again, shook his head, and snorting, stopped to within a few feet of me, facing and watching. He'd thought me responsible for the fall he'd just had, and that he'd get another if he tried to break away from me again.

Where he'd got that education was that, along with other happenings we'd had, and the one of just a few days before where he'd took such a slide and hard fall, he'd come to thinking he'd only get the worst of it by trying to break away. He stood quivering, but plum still then as I walked up to him and slipped my rope over his head.

I WAS AT THAT CAMP about a week when I took it onto myself to turn that cow and calf out and shove 'em to a country where they belonged. Where they ought to've been in the first place. Then I rode on to the main camp where I took on a fresh string of horses and went to riding from other spring camps, where a rider was really needed.

But I kept Joker in with the new string, and I was riding him along one day when I run onto a lanky steer with one horn grown bent and which was gouging into his upper jaw. That steer had been missed in quite a few round-ups or that horn would of been taken care of.

I soon seen why he'd been missed, for he run alone, and soon as he seen me he was gone like a deer, hitting for a thick patch of that brushy country. But this time he was some little distance too far away from it, and before he could get to it my loop caught up with him.

But not as I wanted it to, for instead of catching him by his one straight horn and the head as I intended, the loop sailed down alongside his nose and caught him by one front foot. I didn't know I'd caught him until I pulled up on my slack, and then things happened.

It was an accident and one of the queer ones that happens with roping, but at the speed we all was going down the steep side hill, and I pulling up my slack, that steer upended to a clean turn over. He upended a second time and then as he got to scrambling to his feet, all with no let up in the speed, and neither Joker nor me expecting any such, Joker run right onto that steer's upraised rump, turning him over once more, and as that steer turned over again, Joker and me was also very much upraised by his frame, like from a prop that of a sudden come up, and at the speed we was going we was raised high and to sail on quite a ways before landing.

It was a hard landing, amongst rocks and many kinds of prickly brush. But Joker took the hardest fall, 'cause I know we went to the end of the rope before we got back to earth again. Joker got the sudden jerk of the tied rope which flipped him to land harder. As for me I just went sailing on, to roll over a few times and stop against a nice big boulder.

I looked back to see Joker up, all spooky from the fall. The steer was still down, with his head under him, and I tried to get at Joker before he went to the end of the rope again. But one glance of where it was and I knew what would happen. It happened during that one glance, for, as Joker got to his feet the rope was between his hind legs. As goosy as he always was, especially right then, and as he felt that rope between his hind legs, was all that was needed to stir things some more. He hunched up, made a high buck jump against it and he near fell again, but this time the rope broke near the loop end, snapped back and popped him on the rump—and Joker went from there.

As I seen him go I figured sure I was afoot this time, and so far from camp I didn't dare think about it. I didn't for the time anyway, 'cause the steer drawed my attention. He was now up, wild-eyed

As that steer turned over again, Joker and me
was also very much upraised by his frame.

and looking around, aching to fight anything that moved and run to get at it. I edged to the big boulder on all fours, and as he spotted me it sure didn't take me no time to scramble up on top of it. I felt the breeze of him as he went by and thought sure he'd take a wing off my shaps with his one good horn as I scrambled up.

He didn't go but a few yards when he turned, and seeing me on top of that boulder I thought sure he'd tackle it. I wish he had and I done everything but try to stop him from doing it. But that steer had seen and dodged plenty of boulders before, and shaking his head, like daring me to be fool enough to come down off of it, he blowed on past it again and on he went for the thick and thorny brush where he'd first headed for when my rope upended him. And as he went on that way shaking his head at every shadow as he went, still looking for something to fight, I noticed that that one bum horn of his which had been growing in his jaw, had been broken off in the tumble. The work I wanted to do was done, and like yanking off a bad tooth and more, he'd now soon be all right.

I watched him go, and knowing he wouldn't return for some time I climbed down from the boulder and started on the way Joker had stampeded, not with any thought of ever finding or catching up with him, only he'd gone the direction of camp, the closest water, and a good many miles away. All I thought of was they'd sure be long ones.

I took off my shaps, throwed 'em over my back to keep the sun off, also not to hinder my walking, and as I started it was in no running walk but one set to last for some long distance, and to make it.

It was one of the very few times in my life I'd ever been set afoot. The ones before had been where I'd have to make just a few strides, and it looked like this time would sure make up for them, also any others that might come later on.

Being so all set to make the distance, I was near disappointed when going around a ledge, and not over half mile from where the steer had been well stopped, I seen Joker a-standing there and like he was petrified.

I stood sort of petrified too, and wondering what the samhill could have stopped and was holding him. I didn't stand petrified long, and at the sight of him my disappointment soon went the opposite as I unlimbered myself towards him.

He seen me at about the same time I did him, and he didn't budge. His head was the wrong way from where he'd started. He'd turned around and seemed fixed at watching something on the ground in front of him.

I eased up then, and near had to laugh as I came near and seen what he'd been watching and seemed to hold him. It was the broken end of the rope which had got between his legs during the fall and snapped at him as he'd got up and stampeded. In his running the rope had whipped to one side and he'd turned to face it, afraid to move, for fear of getting another fall and pop on the rump.

Thinking it might spook him to another start I didn't pick up the end of the rope as I came near him. Instead I just took hold of the bridle reins, then the rope, and I never seen such a show of relaxing as I did on that horse after I'd coiled up what was left of that rope and hung it safe up on the saddle and out of his way.

That was another joke on Joker, for, even tho it wouldn't of done him no good at the end of the long run, he could easy kept on going. Many good and well broke rope horses would have, but I was mighty glad Joker had got to thinking he'd better not.

Joker played many jokes on himself and his rider that way, seldom with his knowing or meaning to. He was all life and go, and played jokes when free and amongst other horses. He was a born joker.

XIV

HORSES I'LL NEVER FORGET

W ITH THESE STORIES OF some horses I've known I sure will have to chip in a few words in remembrance of good old Smoky, Big-Enough, also the cream of horseflesh I now have to take their place. This one I named Cortez, after the Spanish Conquistador, who brought our first horses by way of Mexican shores, the finest of Moorish horses, only about sixteen of 'em. As they multiplied, some getting away was the foundation breed of our wild horse, the "Mesteno" which thru some centuries spread from Mexico into the southwest. Many of the best to be rode, up and bred in Old California, Oregon, and on up to British Columbia.

Some of the strains was kept up to standard, named and recorded, and, far as I can gather this Cortez horse of mine is of the Comet strain, one of the earliest, from Mexico into southwest Texas.

A few of them was with a bunch that was shipped up onto my ranch in Montana some years ago, and there Cortez was foaled and raised. He broke out to be a natural cowhorse, with brains that would make a human wonder. Like with Smoky, he can sense from as far as he can see me, by my actions or tone of voice, as to just how I feel and whether, if he's to be rode, it's to be just to pasear, rest or play, or work, and he willingly bows his crested neck to whatever is up. He's up to anything I feel like doing, from quiet riding to heading off an eagle attacking a mountain goat's kid, or roping a steam engine, if I so wished to try.

He's one horse, along with Smoky and Big-Enough, that I never fought or let out a cuss word to. That wasn't and is not called for with such as them. I've fought judheads, stiff-necked, know-nothing, and don't-want-to-know horses, wise, scheming outlaws, as Smoky once was, when he was named *The Cougar*. Then he was stolen and turned to be the outlaw he was. Cortez has the same look in his eye as Smoky did. Kind, but can turn just the opposite in a flash. He's suspicious of strangers, and even tho being no sugar-eating pet, always looks 'em over, over my shoulder and seldom lets any of 'em touch him. Not trained, just his caliber.

Smoky was of a fighting breed, from a cross which at them times I didn't bother or even think of tracing. The only thing I was satisfied with was that he was all horse. The same with this Cortez horse which is a mighty close duplicate of him in every way excepting color. Cortez is a dark, dappled brown, with bald face speckled as tho it'd been splashed at with a paint brush. He broke much easier than Smoky did, but his temperament is the same and if aggravated he could turn to as wicked an outlaw as Smoky was, for he has the same cougarlike action, which is smooth and still can be so quick and swift.

I sure won't give him no cause to make use of that action, only to the good that's in him, like with handling stock which he so enjoys and is such a top at, or maybe just plain riding which he also enjoys, for, with his interest in everything he sees, even the same trails are always new to him.

He's now eight years old, and with the good care I give him, free to roam from clover pasture to stable as he wishes, for shelter during

The only thing I was satisfied with was that he was all horse.

storms or for relief from flies or heat, never tied in a stall, he ought to be sound and in as fine shape as he is now for at least twenty-five years more.

I don't ride him near as much as he'd like me to, not enough to have to keep him shod or at all get him sore footed. So there won't be no pinching shoes contracting his feet, causing corns and such. I keep his hoofs trimmed, not too close, and sometimes melt some tar and daub the bottom of 'em for a protection when the ground is dry and hard. Besides being protecting, that's good toughening and healing stuff to apply, whether the horse is sore footed or not.

With all this kind of treatment this horse ought to live twice the age old Smoky did, for that horse's poor care and abuse after he'd quit as a bucking horse sure told on him and was the cause of his much too early death.

Smoky wasn't my own horse. I only broke him for the outfit I was riding for at the time, but he'd just as well been my own for there was only one unsuccessful try at some one else riding him while I had him with the outfit, and none when I found him again after he'd been stolen and I cared for him until he laid down for his last sleep.

I'd kept him hid away for myself as I broke him and when riders come to take away the broncs I'd "started." I'd run in bunch after bunch of broncs, "started" (took the rough off of 'em) and turned 'em over to other riders for final education with cow work . . . all the time keeping Smoky hid, when, according to outfits' rules, I should of turned him in along with the other started broncs.

Mentioning the outfit where Smoky was foaled and raised I will only say that at one time, when I was riding for it, it had cow camps and headquarters spreading in most every western state from Mexico to Canada. Any of the cowboys who rode for that outfit at that time will know which outfit I mean, even tho there was others just as big.

For a identifying clue, that widespread outfit about lost all their cattle, many many thousands in one year, and went to raising horses.

That outfit had many horses when I rode for them and broke Smoky. They soon forgot about him when he was stolen and never knew of his turning outlaw, but I did, and there was only a remnant of him when I found him again, brought him back to life and took care of him until he looked like a horse again. I never rode him after I found him again. It took him a long while, but he finally got to recognize me again, after many years of being a top arena bucking horse and outlaw, down to a junk wagon horse.

In the meantime the outfit who owned him changed hands now and then and dwindled until now what's left of it is scattered in some southwestern states, close to the Border. They wouldn't of wanted Smoky again after I found him, even if they'd known of him and who had him, for he was past much use and would of brought very little if sold. They wouldn't of sold him anyway, just pensioned him for the good cowhorse he'd once been and good work he'd done.

I buried him deep in the desert where he'd come to camp and died near me. He was fat as a seal as he laid down and like just went to sleep without even flinching or blinking an eye lid as he drew his last breath.

I had another Smoky horse practically given to me by the foreman of a cow outfit neighboring mine, but that horse was a Smoky only in color and markings. He didn't have the fine build, action, or near the brains good old Smoky had. He was a head shaking, prancing nut that didn't turn out to be much of a cowhorse. He could stand long and hard rides tho, but I never rode him once myself, for I sure have no use for any head shaking prancing horse and I kept him as just one of the saddle horses for any of my riders on the ranch.

For my own use, being my work was a heap more to writing and drawing than to riding, I kept only two horses. My favorite then, before Cortez was old enough to break in, was a little solid bay I named Big-Enough. A name which sure fitted him, for he sure belied his size, for speed, strength and endurance, and all around top little cowhorse, cool-headed and with a good set of brains, and big enough for anything that could be expected of any good cowhorse. He weighed around nine hundred pounds when he was fat, and he of course was always fat. He's now in his thirties and still in good shape, quite a ripe old age for a horse considering that the average length of a horse's life is about eighteen.

Big-Enough was the one who figured in my book by that name. What all I wrote of him in that book is all very true as to his character and caliber. He never was very much for bucking, not even after running free in tall grass for months. About the only time he'd bog his head (buck) some was when first saddled and he'd be started too quick. Rut that'd be more like in play with him then, not with any meanness, and when I'd line him out to work he was always all interest and serious.

With him, for some years, I used another horse, another top cowhorse named Booger. He'd been in many parts of the U.S.A., from the Rockies where he was foaled and raised to New York,

*About the only time he'd bog his head some was when
first saddled and he'd be started too quick.*

Texas, and other points far and wide. He was even to Europe a few times, for Booger was a great rope horse and he was taken to rodeos most everywhere where there was any, and used in roping contests. He was also used in bull-dogging contests to pack his rider alongside the fast running steer, to within reach of the long horns which the contestant would grab, swing out of the saddle to the side of the steer's neck, and with his hold on the horns, twisting the steer's neck at the same time skipping for a foot hold with pointed heels, check the steer to a stop then throw him flat to his side.

A fast and good cowhorse is mighty important to get to the steer quick as possible, for with bull-dogging, like with roping, all such events are decided on by time. The shortest time made declares the winner.

Booger, being a three-quarter thoroughbred, was good and fast. He had the good weight of about ten hundred and fifty for good active and roping purposes. That was old Smoky's weight also, maybe a little closer to eleven hundred. With Cortez his weight is over eleven hundred, plenty heavy for a saddle horse, but all of that seems to be to his advantage for he can handle any part of himself as well as any good quick smaller horse can, and with that long, natural and far reaching stride of his, without effort, makes most horses have to jog in order to keep up with him at a walk.

I could add on much more about these horses I've just mentioned, even if I've already written a whole book on the life of Smoky and another on Big-Enough. Both under their names for titles.

I've also used them horses' good points and happenings with them to sort of fit in with stories where such would go well, and credited to some other horses by other names. I will write some more of them along with other stories where I can use more of their good traits to good advantage.

About these other horses I've written of in this book they're only a few of the many more *Horses I've Known*. These just sort of stood out from others in my memory on account of their odd characters, and happenings and experiences brought on by their queer acting and doings,

I'll always remember many horses, especially the ones I have tied down in print and sort of record in this book. But the one standing above all other horses I've known in my memory, one which I'll sure never forget and went to the top in whatever he done, to the good or the bad, is Old Smoky, that good mouse colored, bald faced and stocking legged perfect horse.

Big-Enough comes next, and even tho I haven't ridden him for some years and won't ever ride him again, I'll always think all of him that he deserves, which is aplenty.

And now comes another perfect horse, Cortez, to take the place of them two and keep me from missing them too much. He has all the qualities and beauty that the other two was so well stocked with, and he's to be with me to go on for a long, long time, in both riding and writing, and some day to come, if I don't use him all up, piece by piece, to fit in in part with stories of other horses, I will want to write a book of his life too, after he's lived some more.

He's to be with me to go on for a long, long time.

W ill James was born Joseph Ernest Nephtali Dufault in the province of Quebec on June 6, 1892. He left home as a teenager to live out his dream of becoming a cowboy in the American West. James went on to write and illustrate twenty-four books and numerous magazine articles about horses, cowboying, and the West. His works soon captured the imagination of the public. He died in 1942, at the age of fifty.

We encourage you to patronize your local bookstore. Most stores will order any title that they do not stock. You may also order directly from Mountain Press using the order form provided below or by calling our toll-free number and using your MasterCard or VISA. We will gladly send you a complete catalog upon request.

Other fine Will James Titles:

_____	Cowboys North and South	14.00/paper	25.00/cloth
_____	The Drifting Cowboy	16.00/paper	
_____	Smoky, the Cowhorse	16.00/paper	36.00/cloth
_____	Cow Country	14.00/paper	
_____	Sand	16.00/paper	30.00/cloth
_____	Lone Cowboy	16.00/paper	30.00/cloth
_____	Sun Up	18.00/paper	
_____	Big-Eough	16.00/paper	
_____	Uncle Bill	14.00/paper	26.00/cloth
_____	All in the Day's Riding	16.00/paper	
_____	The Three Mustangeers	15.00/paper	30.00/cloth
_____	Home Ranch	16.00/paper	30.00/cloth
_____	Young Cowboy		15.00/cloth
_____	In the Saddle with Uncle Bill	14.00/paper	26.00/cloth
_____	Scorpion, A Good Bad Horse	15.00/paper	30.00/cloth
_____	Cowboy in the Making		15.00/cloth
_____	Flint Spears, Cowboy Rodeo Contestant	15.00/paper	30.00/cloth
_____	Look-See with Uncle Bill	14.00/paper	26.00/cloth
_____	The Will James Cowboy Book		18.00/cloth
_____	The Dark Horse	18.00/paper	35.00/cloth
_____	Horses I've Known	20.00/paper	
_____	My First Horse		16.00/cloth
_____	The American Cowboy	18.00/paper	
_____	Will James' Book of Cowboy Stories		30.00/cloth

Please include $3.00 per order to cover postage and handling.

Please send the books marked above. I have enclosed $ _____

Name_____

Address _____

City/State/Zip _____

☐ Payment enclosed (check or money order in U.S. funds)

Bill my: ☐ VISA ☐ MasterCard Expiration Date: _____

Card No _____

Signature_____

MOUNTAIN PRESS PUBLISHING COMPANY
P. O. Box 2399 · Missoula, Montana 59806
Order Toll-Free **1-800-234-5308** · _Have your MasterCard or VISA ready_
e-mail: info@mtnpress.com · website: www.mountain-press.com

Printed in the United States
212365BV00002B/1/P